Rania Ropes a Rancher

Rania Ropes a Rancher

Rania Hamner and her family emigrated from Sweden fourteen years ago to work on a Texas ranch, working cattle and herding them up the Chisholm Trail. Something in her life on the trail caused her to doubt her worth, and her ability to trust a man enough to become his wife. Once the family buys a homestead in Kansas, she meets a rancher who begins to make her believe she can trust and fall in love after all.

Rancher Jacob Wilerson noticed Rania last year when she rode drag behind a herd of longhorns—right down Main Street of Ellsworth, Kansas. He's been waiting for her family to return this spring with another Texas herd to the booming cowtown, because he hopes to rope her into staying permanently on his ranch—the way she had already roped his heart.

When Rania's past attacks with new danger, she decides to fight for all she's worth because she realizes she wants to be with Jacob forever.

When Jacob realizes Rania is in danger, he rushes to save her, whether or not she still loves him, hoping to rope Rania—his heart—once more, as she has roped his.

Rania Ropes a Rancher

Linda K. Hubalek

Butterfield Books Inc.

Lindsborg, Kansas

Rania Ropes a Rancher: A Historical Western Romance
Brides with Grit Series: Book 1

Copyright © 2014 by Linda K. Hubalek

Book ISBN-13: 978-1502827098

Library of Congress Control Number: 2014918670

Cover photo: This antique wedding photo is from the author's great grandparent's wedding album. There was no name or date on back of the photo.

Printed in the United States of America.

All rights reserved. Without limiting the right under copyright reserved above, no part of this publication may be reproduced, stored in or introduced into a retrieval system, or transmitted, in any form, or by any means (electronic, mechanical, photocopying, recording, or otherwise) without the prior written permission of both the copyright owner and the publisher, Butterfield Books Inc. The only exception is by a reviewer, who may quote short excerpts in a review.

This book is a work of fiction. Except for the history of Ellsworth, Kansas that has been mentioned in the book, the names, characters, places, and incidents either are the product of the author's imagination or are used fictitiously, and any resemblance to actual persons, living or dead, business establishments, events, or locales is entirely coincidental.

For an order blank for the Butterfield Books' series, please look in the back of this book, or log onto http://butterfieldbooks.com./

Retailers, Libraries and Schools: Books are available at discount rates through Butterfield Books Inc., or your book wholesaler.

To contact the author, or the publisher *Butterfield Books Inc.* please email to staff@butterfieldbooks.com or write to PO Box 407, Lindsborg, KS 67456.

DEDICATION

To ranch women, past and present—
You are the *heart* of the Ranch.

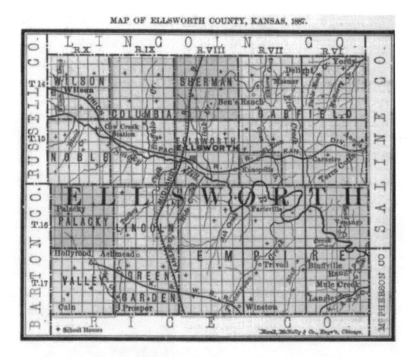

1887 map of Ellsworth County, Kansas.

Books By Linda K. Hubalek

Butter in the Well Series
Butter in the Well

Prairie Bloomin'

Egg Gravy

Looking Back

Trail of Thread Series
Trail of Thread

Thimble of Soil

Stitch of Courage

Planting Dreams Series
Planting Dreams

Cultivating Hope

Harvesting Faith

Kansas Quilter Series
Tying the Knot

Patching Home (2015 release)

Piecing Memories (2015 release)

Brides with Grit Series
Rania Ropes a Rancher

Millie Marries a Marshal

Hilda Hogties a Horseman

PROLOGUE

May 2, 1872, Ellsworth, Kansas

Jacob Wilerson stood on the dusty boardwalk on the north side of South Main in Ellsworth, marveling at how the town had changed in the five years since the town's birth. Wooden buildings of all sizes and shapes, mostly with false fronts, mixed in with a few brick establishments like the bank on the corner. *The Ellsworth Café. Miller's Livery. Homestead Hotel.* Bold painted signs hanging above the business door or painted on the front of the buildings. The first businesses sprang up overnight in tents and shacks. Some of them are long gone, but other businesses have taken their space. The dirt streets—once an original carpet of prairie grass—varies from muddy ruts, hard-packed snow and ice, to hot powdery dust, depending on the weather conditions and time of year.

There wasn't a tree in sight; buildings just cropped up on the prairie with the wide–open sky as a backdrop.

Jacob was fourteen, ten years ago, when his folks brought their young family out to the virgin prairie of the Kansas Territory to escape the Civil War. He and his older brother Adam and

Rania Ropes a Rancher

younger sibling, Noah, each a year apart from Jacob, were at the age they would soon be pulled into the war if they didn't leave civilization behind.

They left Illinois and kept traveling west, past the Kansas and Missouri border problems, to central Kansas. His father Moses filed a claim on homestead land between the Clear Creek and the Smoky Hill River, two miles south of the Butterfield Overland Route that ran from Kansas City to Denver. But within a few years, forts were established along this same route to handle the Indian uprisings. Fort Harker was built two miles west of their claim and Ellsworth five miles further west. Now their peaceful, private prairie teemed with businesses, people and more cattle than a person could ever imagine—because now the railroad traveled across the prairie too, bringing civilization with it.

Of course his family had changed, too. Adam was now the marshal for the little town called Clear Creek north of their ranch. Adam said he was never going to marry because of his chosen profession. Noah homesteaded the land next to his parents and was writing to a girlfriend back in Illinois.

Jacob had taken charge of the original land when his father died three years ago. His mother Cate and sister Sarah still lived with him. He was marrying age, twenty-four, but hadn't met the right woman yet to take on ranch life.

Jacob didn't mind being close to towns and supplies. It made life easier, and hopefully would bring more women and families this way. Even though the extra cattle that the drives brought up each spring brought good income to town, it also brought noise, smell and ruckus when herds—and cowboys—got riled.

The herds grazed south of town and used the river as their water source, until it was time to load them onto the trains heading

Brides with Grit

to the Eastern states. Groups were brought across the river and down the street to the pens and chutes that would load the animals onto railroad cars.

Right now the noise—and dust level—rose as a new herd trotted right down South Main Street. Everyone scattered out of the street when they heard the rhythm of the hooves hitting the packed dirt heading for the rail yards. It was beginning to be an everyday occurrence as thirty thousand head of cattle were expected to arrive and ship out of Ellsworth over the next few months. That's a lot of dust, mud and manure.

Abilene was once the main cowtown, but drovers switched to Ellsworth this year as the train tracks went farther west now, and the Abilene businessmen and area ranchers were tired of the giant herds and Texas Fever cattle disease that encompassed Dickinson County spring through fall. There were around forty thousand cattle shipped out of Abilene last year, and Jacob couldn't fathom that many longhorns roaming around Ellsworth County this summer—but they were starting to arrive.

The cattle streamed past Jacob's view in a river of dust and color, kept in line by the front leader and side riders. A group of ten cowboys could handle a twenty-five hundred head herd, and so far Jacob had counted six riders. Foot and wagon traffic was put on hold for several minutes, and horses tied to the hitching posts along the edges of the boardwalks crowded up against the posts, warily watching the horns as they passed.

As the last of the herd went alongside, Jacob noticed the cowboy riding drag. As the dust thinned, Jacob saw a split skirt on the rider instead of trousers. It was unusual to see a woman riding drag, but she appeared confident and capable in the job.

Rania Ropes a Rancher

Actually, all he saw of the woman on the side facing him was a thick layer of dried mud coating her body and the horse's. It looked as though she and her palomino paint took a wild slide down the river bank while herding the livestock across the river. Between her wide-brimmed hat pushed low on her forehead, and a bandana covering her face, Jacob couldn't even see her eyes. When the woman passed, he saw a waist–length blonde braid down her back—and even it was muddy.

Jacob snapped his head down the walk as a woman screamed and yelled to someone who was between the two of them. A longhorn bull had done a quick right turn, heading straight to the boardwalk, and toward a frightened child, who was stock still and staring at the giant animal.

Before Jacob could run down the twenty feet to the little boy, the horsewoman tailing the herd, snapped a lasso through the air which landed around the six-foot spread of the bull's horns. She yanked the rope back hard with her right, gloved hand at the same time her horse jumped backwards, snapping the animal's head back from its disastrous route. Both bull and boy were bawling at once, but the horse and rider just pulled the animal back onto the route of the herd, like it was an everyday occurrence. The woman was attuned to the livestock, but she also saw the child in danger in an instant, and took care of both.

Now that's the kind of wife he needed, someone who could ride, rope, handle livestock and children—a woman with grit—and Jacob wondered if this particular one was married or single.

4

CHAPTER 1

April 26, 1873, near Clear Creek, Ellsworth County, Kansas

Jacob Wilerson whipped his head to the west when he heard the shrill call from a horse somewhere in the distance. He touched his knees against the sides of Duncan to halt the buckskin gelding. After the horse's snort of acknowledgement, Jacob cocked his head to listen again for the other horse.

The light breeze and warm sunshine made a perfect spring day for the leisurely ride home the two of them were having on their return from the Cross C Ranch. Jacob was lost in thought about the string of horses he just delivered to the neighboring rancher six miles east of them. He wasn't paying attention to his surroundings while they roamed along the small canyon above the banks of the Smoky Hill River.

His eyes, shaded by the wide–brimmed hat, scanned the fresh, green, waving grass of the Kansas prairie, trying to locate the distressed horse. The prairie birds' trills, which had blended in with the whispering movement of the grass, stopped abruptly like they were listening too.

Rania Ropes a Rancher

The other horse neighed loudly again, enabling Jacob's ears to pin the direction it came from. Jacob's right hand touched the reins on Duncan's neck to turn the horse toward the danger while the other pulled his rifle out of the saddle's scabbard. He'd been caught daydreaming, which was never a smart thing for a lone rider to do out on the open prairie.

He nudged Duncan slowly forward until he could see the other horse's head over the top of the sloping edge of the canyon. Easing forward in the saddle, he could see a palomino paint prancing in place; its reins seemed to be held firmly down to the ground.

The Hamner family from Texas came to mind because they bred and sold this crossbreed of horses. Jacob had heard the Hamners were back in the area with their latest cattle drive, but he hadn't seen them yet. He was also excited to hear they bought the nearby Larson ranch to live here permanently.

Jacob scanned the area again, looking for another horse, person, or movement in the rocky cropping above the scene. But all seemed quiet except for the agitated horse.

Just then the horse moved, and Jacob spied a light–colored sleeve hanging mid–air clinging to the rein that was keeping the horse from trotting off. Lying on the ground, dangerously close to the prancing hoofs, lay a still body, half hidden in the new growth of grass.

"Ha," Jacob hoarsely whispered to push Duncan forward, while still scanning the area for unseen trouble. Duncan perked up his ears as he smelled the mare and eagerly closed the distance between them. The tall mare released a shudder of relief that they had been found, but moved warily between him and her rider. Jacob knew the mare wanted to raise her head higher and be ready

Brides with Grit

to attack as they got closer, but yet she respected the reins hold of her unconscious rider.

Jacob stopped Duncan twenty feet away and slowly swung his right leg over the saddle, quietly dropping his feet to the ground. He dropped his horse's reins, thus silently telling Duncan to stay where he stood. Jacob cocked his rifle and slowly walked around Duncan who had been shielding Jacob, in case the person on the ground swung a loaded revolver toward them.

Jacob took one slow step at a time, glancing between the mare and the person on the ground. "Whoa there, horse. It's okay. I just want to help your rider."

The horse pranced around and Jacob was scared the horse's hooves would step on…the woman.

A thick blonde braid lay sprawled across the grass, probably exactly where it landed after flying through the air when the woman was unseated from the saddle. She was lying on her right side, toward Jacob, with her head resting on her right arm. Her elevated left hand was wrapped around a single rein, keeping the mare close behind her body. Jacob studied her chest, whispering a prayer of thanks when he saw it was still moving with her breaths. Her wide–brimmed hat lay a few feet away where it fell when she took the tumble from her horse.

The woman wore a light brown spilt skirt, cream–colored shirtwaist and an unbuttoned men's style, brown wool vest with lots of front pockets. A trickle of blood crossed her forehead, slowly seeping onto her shirt sleeve below her head.

Did she get shot, or hit her head when she fell? As the horse flitted around, light caught the glint of fresh blood on the seat of the saddle. Maybe she was hurt before she slid out of the saddle?

7

Rania Ropes a Rancher

Jacob's eyes widened with recognition. He'd first seen that distinctive swatch of blonde hair a year ago when a trail drive came into Ellsworth. He remembered this horse and rider, both covered with mud, were riding in drag behind the herd of Texas longhorns.

Later that same day, he'd met and passed her walking with two other women on the Main Street boardwalk. He was conversing with his brother Adam, and wasn't paying any attention to who else was sharing the walk until they passed the women. Jacob glanced back to see the three wore similar large, slouch hats; the older woman wore a long skirt; one of the younger women sported men's trousers; and this one, a half foot taller than the other two, was wearing a split skirt, although most of the caked mud had been brushed off. You could tell all three were related, but their different personalities showed by their choice of attire. Jacob had guessed it was a mother and her two daughters in their early twenties.

The woman in trousers then walked backwards to watch him and Adam, smiling and waving until the older woman tugged her sleeve to turn back around. The other young woman peeked more discretely over her shoulder at them, and smiled when she saw Jacob staring at her. Just then Jacob's feet boots faltered, causing him to fall off the boardwalk into a pile of horse turds. Adam laughed so hard he could barely lend a hand to help Jacob out of the smelly mess.

By chance and luck, Jacob worked with her family, the Hamners, for a couple of weeks while sorting their cattle at the Ellsworth rail yards. Jacob hired on with the railroad to work during the cattle drive season to supplement his ranch income.

The Hamner parents, Oskar and Annalina—and all the siblings: Leif, Dagmar, Rania and her twin Hilda—were proficient

8

Brides with Grit

riders and stock handlers. The Swedish immigrants worked well as a team, rarely calling out to each other because they sensed one another's motions.

How he wished he could see that sweet Swedish smile spread across her pretty face now. He had missed Rania when the family left for Texas, and he'd been eagerly anticipating her return this spring, especially with the news that they were permanently moving to the area. Jacob's heart missed several beats seeing her like this—because she was the woman he had recently decided to court now that she would live nearby.

Jacob slowly walked a wide circle around the horse, trying to get the mare's attention and her hooves away from the woman. Her perked ears and eyes followed his every movement, wary of Jacob's presence. The horse finally jerked the reins out of the rider's gloved hand and edged toward Duncan. Jacob slowly walked toward the woman, keeping an eye on the horse in case it whirled toward him.

Jacob knelt down, placing a hand on the arm that had fallen with the loss of the rein. "Miss Hamner? Can you hear me? Rania?" Jacob's soft words caused the woman's light blue eyes to flutter open, but they had a glazed, confused look before closing again. She drew her shoulders and arm forward in a wince, and brushed her left hand across her forehead, spreading a smear of blood from a cut there into her fair hair. Then she moved her hand to cup her abdomen, her face grimacing as she did so.

Jacob leaned over Rania, slowly and gently running his hands over her limbs and trunk, feeling for any broken bones, but not finding anything obvious. Jacob blew out his held breath, relieved that there were no obvious breaks, but you never know when a person is unconscious.

Rania Ropes a Rancher

"Miss Hamner? I just found you here on the ground. Did you get bucked off?" Jacob gulped when she turned onto her back and he saw spots of blood on her skirt between her legs. *Oh no.* Did the horse step on her after she had fallen? How would he move her if she had a crushed pelvis? He closed his eyes and swallowed hard, thinking about the pain this poor woman could be enduring.

But then he looked back at her horse and remembered there was already blood on the saddle.

"No." Jacob could hardly hear her faint word, so he leaned over her head to hear her better. Her eyes were still squeezed shut. "I slid to the ground when I was blacking out."

Jacob sat up on his heels, letting out a breath of relief, but he still had a distressed woman to help.

"Well looks like you cut your head landing on a rock…and something else is going on, too. Think you can handle me getting you back into the saddle? I can ride behind you and get you into town to see the doctor."

Her hand moved from her abdomen to put her palm up in the air as a signal to stop him. "No! I can't go anywhere until this is over, and I can't be seen by the doctor or my family."

"Well Miss Hamner, I can't leave you lying out in the open prairie like this. You need help and you're going to get it."

When her light–blue eyes opened and searched his for understanding, Jacob caught her recognition of him.

"Are you the marshal?" That whispered line pulled her hand back from his.

Well, that's just great, I want to court her and she doesn't know who I am? "No, I'm Jacob Wilerson. You're thinking of my

10

Brides with Grit

brother Adam, the marshal in Clear Creek. We both have light brown hair, mustaches and look somewhat similar—I guess."

Jacob hesitated, then continued, "I helped your family at the Ellsworth rail pens last year, sorting and loading cattle onto the trains…" *And I thought of you for the whole year since.*

"Oh, now I know which Wilerson you are…the one who asked questions all the time." Rania's body relaxed a bit so she must have remembered his attention and bantering with her last year. And it was good to see she had her senses about her, not totally befuddled after she hit her head.

"Well, what's going on if you didn't get stepped on?"

Her pale face blushed to bright pink and she grimaced when another wave of pain seemed to hit her body and she clutched her abdomen again.

Now Jacob's suntanned face turned white with the thought of something feminine going on in front of him. "Uh… is it time for your monthly?" He looked back to her horse and realized there weren't any saddle bags, so no chance of her having any bleeding rags or change of clothing with her.

Jacob snapped out of his embarrassing thoughts because she was injured and needed help. "Look, I'm going to move you down by the river's edge. There's a cottonwood down there that will give us a little shade. Then I'll get my extra shirt out of my saddle bag and…try to stop the bleeding."

"No way are you going to stop it," she hissed through her clinched lips. "I want this…blood out of me now."

Jacob fell back on his seat, because her venomous words caught him by surprise. *Now what should I do?*

11

Rania Ropes a Rancher

Help her out. His ma's words rang through his head like she had just slapped his forehead. Without hesitation, Jacob moved down on one knee and gently gathered Rania up in his arms. He hefted her against his chest, standing up and getting his balance while holding her weight. She started to protest, but Jacob's arms held her tight against his chest, giving her no room to fight even if she wanted to. Rania, at six feet, was as tall as Jacob, so it was work to carry her the twenty yards across the grass and down the slope to the base of a cottonwood tree.

Rania's body tightened when another wave of pain hit her as Jacob laid her on the grass, but then she relaxed when it passed. She blew out a breath of air from her puffed cheeks, blinked her eyes several times, and then kept them open because she was in shade now instead of the glaring sun.

Now that Rania was moved, Jacob went back for the horses. It was easy to catch the reins on Duncan, but Rania's horse waltzed just out of reach for a few minutes until Jacob caught one rein by luck when she threw her head back. Jacob tugged on the reins and both horses obediently followed him down to the cottonwoods and nearby brush along the riverbank. He tied their reins on some scrubby plum bushes a few yards from where he had left Rania. Next, he opened up the flap on his leather saddlebag, pulled out his extra shirt and threw it over his shoulder. His water canteen, slung across the saddle pommel, was still full from when he left the other ranch, so Jacob slung its strap over his other shoulder. Lastly he unhooked his bedroll from the back of the saddle. Rania could use his blanket to either lie on, or shield her body from his sight, but he intended to help her, whether she liked it or not.

Rania blew more air and opened her eyes when she heard him nearby again.

"Is Rose okay?"

Brides with Grit

"Your horse? Yeah, although she was a bit hard to catch."

"My brothers call her 'a hard–headed woman' but she and I get along just fine." Jacob was glad to see the bit of a smile on her lips when she talked about her horse.

"Want a little water?" She nodded, so Jacob uncapped the canteen, and then kneeled down beside Rania to gently lift her head. Some of the lukewarm water ran down her face and neck when the canteen was brought to Rania's lips, but she greedily drank the water until Jacob pulled it away. After a few seconds Jacob gave her another drink before laying her head back on the grass.

"Want to lie on my bedroll, or at least put it under your head?" Rania shut her eyes, gripped her abdomen again and nodded negatively.

"How come you're out here by yourself? Any idea how long you been lying unconscious?"

Jacob shook his head in exasperation when she didn't answer because he knew she was still awake. "Come on, Miss Hamner. I can't help if you don't let me know what's going on."

Trying to keep his temper down, Jacob pulled his handkerchief from his back pocket, uncapped the canteen again to drizzle some of the water on the cloth. Rania jerked away when she felt him lay the wet cloth on her forehead. What he really wanted to do was wipe away the tears causing wet streaks down her dusty face, but thought the woman would really have a fit if he tried.

Jacob couldn't figure out why she didn't want his help—well other than it seemed she had a female problem she was embarrassed about. He lived with his mother and sister so he knew what went on with women during their time, and in truth, they could get a little touchy then too.

The water seemed to revive Rania. Her eyes opened and focused on the tree above them, and she took some deep, calming breaths. Jacob rolled up his shirt and tossed it onto her stomach. She didn't meet his eyes as she pushed the wadded shirt between her thighs.

Thinking it would be better to avoid the obvious problem, Jacob decided to ask some other questions—in a roundabout way. "I was happy to hear your folks bought the Larson place on the west side of us. We sure hated losing young Sam, but we are glad your family will be our new neighbors." Jacob tried not to shudder thinking how he found his friend that morning two months ago. Sam had been thrown from his horse, but his foot got caught in the stirrup and his horse drug him back to its home barn. Jacob thanked the Lord he hadn't found Rania in the same shape.

After Sam's death, Jeb Henderson, the local lawyer, contacted Sam's family who lived in Indiana. Sam's father wired back to sell the place "as–is" and wire him the money. Sam's funeral and burial was conducted with his neighbors in attendance, without his family's presence.

Out of curtesy—to the livestock rather than to Sam's missing family—Jacob took care of Sam's animals until they were sold. All farm equipment went with the homestead so no separate auction took place. Rania's parents, who had traveled back and forth between Texas and Kansas for several years, decided they were ready to settle down and bought Larson's ranch. The Hamners were at the right place at the right time to get a good deal.

Rania didn't make any comment yet, so Jacob tried again. "Is your family getting settled in?"

Brides with Grit

After a long pause she finally gave in. "No, my parents and Leif just left on the train this morning for Texas to sell what belongings remained down there. They'll trail back with another outfit with more cattle and the rest of our horse herd."

"Why didn't you go along?"

"It was decided that Dagmar, Hilda and I would stay here to get the place in shape."

"Now that you're talking to me, why don't you tell me why you're out here alone?"

Her cramping pains seemed to have lessened and she moved her hand from her stomach to across her eyes. She sighed before answering. "Dagmar heard about the foreman job at the Bar E Ranch and took off that direction to check on it."

"And your twin?"

"Hilda went to the county land office in Ellsworth to see if there was any land available for sale. She got set in her mind that she wants her own home. And I decided to take a ride to get familiar with the area."

Jacob wet the handkerchief again and reached to wipe her face but still, Rania grimaced and tried to withdraw from his touch. Jacob got an uneasy feeling there was more than just a bad monthly going on with this woman. He draped the wet cloth across her hand so she could wipe her face herself.

He sighed and asked, "What do you want me to do, Miss Hamner? I just want to help you now, and get you back home safely. You might have a concussion so you shouldn't travel by yourself. Plus, I think that cut on your forehead needs to be stitched up."

15

Rania Ropes a Rancher

Rania didn't answer right away, kept taking deep measured breaths, still trying to calm herself. She blew out a slow breath and answered him without opening her eyes. "I can't go home and have Hilda see me like this. Plus I feel like I'll pass out again if I move an inch."

"Okay, maybe we stay here a while in the shade and let you recover. Could we…take off your shirtwaist and skirt and I wash them out in the river? I have a blanket you could cover yourself with."

That comment brought her eyes wide open.

"Well, you said you didn't want Hilda to see you like this…" Jacob tried to reassure her. "It's okay. I have a sister, so I've been around girls before, and my ma brought me up to be a gentleman."

Rania looked like she'd rather crawl in a badger hole and hide instead of let him touch her, let alone remove her clothing.

Jacob sighed and tried another idea. "How about after you rest a while, I take you back to our ranch home and let my mother help you?"

She relaxed, gave a little nod and shut her eyes again, leaving Jacob wondering why he wanted to get involved with this woman when she obviously had issues with trusting men. She didn't seem that way last year.

Yet, feelings for her beat deep in his chest when he looked down on her still body. He felt like this sleeping beauty was the one he'd been waiting for to complete his life, but unfortunately, it looked like there could be obstacles in his way.

***

Brides with Grit

Rania insisted on getting herself in the saddle, and luckily the mare was patient with Rania's weak mounting. Jacob kept a close watch on Rania, noticing that her posture kept deteriorating with every mile they rode. By the time they went three miles to his wooden–framed two–story ranch house, she was clutching the saddle pommel with both hands and her face was awfully pale.

Just as they got to the hitching post by the front door, Rania's chin hit her chest and she started sliding sideways out of the saddle—in the opposite direction of Jacob on his horse.

Jacob jumped off Duncan, sidestepping around the two agitated horses to catch Rania and place her waist gently over his left shoulder before she could fall from the saddle, just as his mother Cate opened the front door." Her long torso and arms extended down his back like an oversized sack of feed. Jacob clutched her knees tightly against his chest to hold her in place. He was attracted to this tall Swedish woman, but right now he wished she was a little petite thing instead.

Cate's eyes flashed wide when his bloodied shirt fell off Rania's backside and draped across Jacob's arms that circled the woman's legs. "Let me put some old towels across my bed and you put her down there," she told him as she left the door wide open for him. Jacob was thankful his mother's bedroom was not upstairs as he eased down the hallway to her room. It would be heck to balance Rania as he walked up the steep, narrow stairs to the bedrooms on the upper floor.

"What happened to her?" Cate burst back in the room with a pitcher of water and towels.

"I found her unconscious a couple of hours ago on the ground near the river. She had a bloody gash on her forehead, besides the

17

other bleeding. Luckily her horse stayed by her, otherwise I never would have seen her lying in the grass."

"What took you so long to bring her here if you found her a while ago?" his mother asked sternly, as she started to unbutton the side buttons of Rania's split skirt. Jacob turned his head to give the women some privacy but didn't leave the room because he needed to answer his mother's questions.

"She woke up for a bit and insisted she just needed to rest. Said she felt faint before blacking out and apparently sliding off her horse. She must have hit her forehead on a rock when she collapsed. I moved her under some trees for shade and a drink of water. We talked a little before getting her back on the horse."

"Well it looks like the woman has a bad monthly or is losing her baby."

Jacob was shocked at his mother's observation. "Uh …this is Miss Rania Hamner, one of the daughters of the couple who just bought the Larson place. I worked with them last year in Ellsworth when they trailed a herd up from Texas. And she was adamant that I not take her to a doctor or home to her family."

"Fine. I'll deal with Rania. You go change your shirt and ride over to the Hamners to let them know Rania's staying overnight."

Jacob looked down and saw Rania's blood smeared on the front of his shirt. It isn't how he hoped his first visit would go with the woman he was interested in courting.

CHAPTER 2

"Hello the house!" Jacob felt strange yelling this to a neighbor's house he had visited many times over the years, but it had changed ownership so he needed to respect the new owners.

Jacob flinched at the constant yelping some insistent little dog was making inside the house. Larson had lived in a sod house for a few years before putting up this wooden–frame structure that now graced the homestead. So far it was a small single–story home, but built ready to add on to the west of the house. Sam had planned to expand the house this spring, but that didn't happen because of his demise. Jacob wondered what Sam would think of the current noisy dog and the new owners.

The door opened and Jacob recognized the young man who lowered his head a bit to clear the doorway so he could step out onto the porch. He had to be over six and a half feet tall. Looks like the first thing this Swedish family needed to do was make the door frames taller.

"Hello. I'm Jacob Wilerson from next ranch over. Your sister Rania is over there with my mother, so I thought I'd let you know."

Rania Ropes a Rancher

Jacob blinked twice when a young woman looking a lot like Rania stepped out behind the man and walked out to stand by Duncan. "We've been worried about Rania when we found she wasn't at home. I didn't think she'd be stopping at one of our new neighbors by herself because she's rather shy.

"Good to see you again, Mr. Wilerson," she continued. "To refresh your memory I'm Rania's sister, Hilda and this is my brother Dagmar. We appreciated your help last year at the Ellsworth rail yard when we sorted and loaded our longhorns."

"Welcome, Mr. Wilerson. I assume you remember which twin is *not* shy?" Hilda looked back at Dagmar smiling when he spoke up. She scrunched her nose at her brother before turning to Jacob. All four siblings had identical blond hair and facial features. Their older brother, Leif was a match in height to Dagmar too. Hilda was a half foot shorter than Rania's six feet. Even if the twins had been identical, you could tell Rania and Hilda apart by their opposite mannerisms. Rania was quiet and reserved, Hilda was chatty and outgoing.

"Why didn't she come with you, Mr. Wilerson?"

"Please call me Jacob. I came across Rania on my way home from the Cross C Ranch east of here. Rania's horse stepped in a hole—or something—and Rania fell off. She had a big gash and goose egg on her forehead that I thought might need stitches. I took Rania to our ranch so my mother could tend to her since it happened nearby.

"I'm sure Rania will be fine with a little rest, but my mother loves to fuss over people. Rania happened to mention you were both gone and not sure when you'd be home, so that cinched the deal for my mother. Rania really has no choice but to stay overnight."

20

Brides with Grit

Jacob hated lying, but it seemed like he had no choice. He'd have to remember the details and repeat them to his mother and Rania to keep the story straight. His mother was wonderful, instead of the pushy person he just made her sound like, but the Hamners would eventually find out that Cate Wilerson would be a good neighbor to them.

Jacob was wracking his brain to make conversation, to make it sound like Rania was sitting and chatting with his mother in their parlor—instead of bleeding in one of their beds. "Dagmar, Rania said you went over to the Bar E Ranch today about the foreman job. Any luck?"

"Yes! Good news, I got the job and I move over to the Bar E house anytime. It's a big ranch, very similar to the Texas ranch near Austin where we've worked. Both ranches have cattle and sheep, so it will be a good fit for me. It sounds like this ranch has had some management problems though."

"Who'd you talk to?" Jacob inquired.

"The owner himself, Mr. Elison. He came from Boston to check on his sons and realized the place was going under with their neglect. He sent the sons back East last week and Mr. Elison stayed here to sort through the mess."

"Well, just so you know what you're getting into. Lyle and Carl Elison were sent out to Kansas because of their expensive habits in Boston, but all they did here was race horses, set up a gambling room in the house and ignore the ranch work. Most of the ranch hands left because they were given no direction—let alone their pay on time."

Dagmar nodded in agreement. "Mr. Elison told me about it, so I'm prepared. He said my father and brother could work there too.

21

That will give me help on the ranch plus provide funds to establish our family ranch.

Hilda interrupted them, "Excuse our manners, Jacob. Our momma would have our heads for not inviting you in for coffee. Please give your horse to Dagmar to put in the barn for a bit, and come into the house." Jacob did as he was bid because he wanted to know more about Rania and her family, even if he had to put up with that yipping dog.

***

The coffee was strong enough to stand a spoon up straight in the cup, and the dried sweet bread hard enough to break a tooth. After Jacob saw Dagmar dip the bread in the coffee before eating it, he tried again and found the bread delicious, melting in his mouth this time. New neighbors, new ways of doing things he surmised. Plus Jacob needed to learn a few Swedish words if he was thinking about courting the immigrants' daughter.

Jacob scanned the kitchen as he sipped his coffee. This room had been cleaned a bit, since they had starting cooking and eating in here recently. Everything in the front room he had walked through was exactly where it had been when Sam left the house the day of his accident. It was kind of eerie to see his things, covered with dust and cobwebs. Rania and Hilda had a lot of cleaning and sorting to do to get the place in shape again.

Besides the front room and kitchen, there were two bedrooms, one larger built for Sam and his intended bride, and one smaller bedroom, for the young children Sam had longed to father one day. Sam planned to add on a parlor, a second story of bedrooms, plus new front and back porches when his family grew.

Brides with Grit

"Thanks for your hospitality, but I should be going," Jacob said as he put on his hat, ready to leave. "I'll ride over with Rania tomorrow to be sure she gets home okay."

Hilda waved a hand at him, "Oh, you don't have to do that. I'll ride over in the morning to ride with Rania. That will give me a chance to meet your mother and sister."

Jacob wracked his brain trying to think of a way to give Rania more time to recuperate before riding again. "My sister Sarah will be home tomorrow afternoon. She's been in Clear Creek this week with her fiancé's family. How about you wait until then and the four of you can have coffee together?" He paused to let Hilda accept, but then came up with a better idea.

"Instead, why don't you and Dagmar come over for supper tomorrow evening at six o'clock? I'll let my brother Adam know we're having a family supper. He'll bring out Sarah's fiancé and you can meet the whole family. See you then." Jacob opened the door and walked out before they had time to say no.

***

Rania moved her head and sighed as the deep feather pillow cushioned her movement. She would have loved to have had a soft pillow like this in her bedroll on the trail. How many months over the years had she slept in a wagon or on the hard ground during their many trips between Texas and Kansas? She really didn't want to know.

She slowly opened her eyes; glad she wasn't on the ground under the open sky. She looked down to the foot of the iron bed, then scanned around the interior of the room to see a large oval mirror on a wooden stand, a polished mahogany chest of drawers, a vanity table, and a row of hooks on the wall where a few dresses hung.

Rania Ropes a Rancher

The delicate lace curtains covering the window to the right of the head of the bed gently fluttered in and out with the breeze coming through the half–opened window. Rania relaxed into the soft sheets again, stroking the smooth cotton that lay beneath her fingers. The pale yellow walls and the pastel patchwork quilt covering her on the bed gave the room a restful but refreshing feel.

She yearned for a bedroom like this. The security and warmth it gave eased some of the fears she'd felt the last few months. Rania was glad her family had decided to settle in one place instead of continuing to make their living herding cattle up the Chisholm Trail. She just hoped the memories of what had happened to her in Texas would fade with time and distance of miles.

A slight knock on the door caused Rania to catch her breath until she thought again of the safety of the room. The doorknob turned and Mrs. Wilerson slowly opened the door and walked the few steps to the bed. "Good morning, Rania. Feeling better? Feel like sitting up and eating something?" Mrs. Wilerson put a cup of tea and a plate of toast on the small table beside the bed.

"Thank you, Ma'am. My headache is down to a dull ache now." Rania didn't mention the other problem she was suffering.

Cate sat down on the edge of the bed and reached for her hands. "Please call me Cate, dear. Those few stitches I put in your gash will hurt even if your forehead wasn't black and blue. I hope you won't have much of a scar. With that large bump on your head it was like mending socks with a darning egg." Cate's shoulders shuddered a bit, probably thinking about what she had to do with her thread and needle yesterday. Next she laughed, trying to lighten their mood, "Guess what I'll think about the next time I darn Jacob's socks?"

Brides with Grit

Cate sighed, searched Rania's face, and squeezed her hands. "Jacob told me I was not to tell your family about your...other bleeding you had earlier, but you can talk to me about it if you want. The conversation won't leave this room." Cate hesitated a moment, and then added, "Last night in your sleep you mumbled something about a baby."

Rania dropped her eyes, and couldn't bring them to meet Cate's. She tried to hold back the tears moistening her lashes, but a tear, then another fell on their hands. Then Rania's pent up emotions burst with the older woman's kind gesture.

"Am I still pregnant since I was bleeding yesterday?" Rania asked the older woman. Surely she'd know and ease Rania's mind.

"I don't know, Rania. Why do you think you're in a family way?"

Rania continued to stare at their locked hands, watching them get wet with her tears. When her nose started to drip, she pulled away, wishing she had a hankie. She would hate to wipe her nose on the nightgown Cate had given her to wear.

"It's okay, honey," Cate gently said as she passed her own handkerchief to Rania. "Take your time, but I think it will help to talk it out. It can't be good to keep it bottled up inside." Cate asked another question when Rania didn't stay a word, "Did you have to leave someone special back in Texas?"

Rania blew an unladylike snot bubble when she snorted on that question. "No." She could guess what her face looked like about now. It always got very red and blotchy when she cried.

It was several moments before she continued. Cate seemed sympathetic and not judgmental, so Rania couldn't help herself from blubbering on. "Poppa hires extra hands to help on the drive.

Rania Ropes a Rancher

About the second week on the trail a new hand started talking to me, bringing me a handful of bluebonnet flowers in the evening. We were behind the wagon where the campfire's shadow didn't reach and I received my first real kiss. I felt so special. I'm so tall and gangly–thin that I look most men in the eye, or down on them. It's usually embarrassing to talk to men, but he didn't make me feel that way."

"Did your love just get out of hand?" Cate asked, not wanting Rania to continue if that was the end of the story.

"He'd suggested we sneak out when everyone was asleep. I thought it was kind of thrilling to get away with it. But when he got me away from the camp, he didn't stop his mouth or hands even when I begged him. He threatened 'accidental deaths' to my family by a stampede or a rifle misfire if I didn't do what he wanted, or if I told anyone." Cate squeezed her hands so hard, that Rania guessed Cate knew what happened that night.

"Did this happen the whole way up here?" Cate whispered in shocked horror.

"No. It ended a couple weeks later when Hilda caught the man with his trousers down when he and I were by the creek, supposedly to fetch water. Between a blow to the side of his head with a tree limb from Hilda, and my momma's cocked gun, he ran off that night. Cowhands sometimes drifted away if they didn't want to work so hard, so we didn't say anything when he disappeared. I'm pretty sure my mother didn't tell my father, because he'd have hunted the man down and shot him, causing my family more trouble than I'm worth."

The older woman drew Rania close to her chest, and soothingly rubbed Rania's back. "Oh young lady, you are so worth being loved and cared for. Don't ever think otherwise."

26

Brides with Grit

Rania pulled away to use the wet hankie again. "I haven't had a monthly since before we left on our trip, I feel faint in the morning, can't fathom eating breakfast…" She paused to blow her nose. "Yesterday I felt sick when out riding and didn't get off the horse fast enough. When I started bleeding, I hoped I was all right and not expecting…but it really wasn't very much."

"Yes, you can still spot a little at first when you're with child. I'm guessing you could still be in a family way then, with your other symptoms. But I'm afraid you won't know for sure until another month. Did you tell your mother or Hilda?" Rania just looked down and shook her head no. "When will your parents be back?"

"It could be six to eight weeks, depending on whether they travel by themselves or hook up with another cattle trail outfit. I'm guessing they'll work their way back up here for the money, though, so it will be July before they're here." Rania paused to draw air, but then her features crumbled with emotional pain. "And I'll be showing by then…"

***

It was good to see the dining room table surrounded by family and friends again. Silverware clicking against china plates, and voices mixed with the steady tock of the wall clock on the fireplace mantel gave a wave of peace to Jacob's soul.

Jacob was glad his mother didn't mind his impromptu idea, because besides Adam, he invited Sarah's fiancé Ethan Freeman, and ranching neighbor, widower Isaac Connely for supper too. He missed seeing his deceased father, Moses and wayward brother, Noah around the table, but that couldn't be helped.

This mixture of new neighbors and old friends made lively conversations around their dining room table. Dagmar and Hilda competed in telling stories, while Rania just smiled and listened. Sarah and Ethan acted more like acquaintances than a couple about to get married. And Isaac and his mother kept glancing and smiling at each other when they thought no one was looking. Hmm. Interesting.

"Men, what's your favorite way to have your potatoes cooked?" All the Wilersons groaned when Jacob asked the question. "What? Questions are a good way to get to know people. Last year when we were together at the rail yards, it was mostly on horseback with a bunch of longhorns between us..."

"Okay. All our ma fixes is boiled potatoes, but these mashed potatoes melt in my mouth, Mrs. Wilerson." Dagmar grinned before digging his fork into the pile of potatoes on his plate. "I now have a new favorite."

"Ma's mashed potatoes are my favorite too, although at home I just cut up and fry a potato in butter before adding eggs to the skillet," was Adam's answer. "Don't want to wash more dishes than I have to since I'm baching."

"And I'm betting you eat right out of the skillet and don't bother putting food on a plate," Cate guessed. Adam just smiled with his mouth full, dearly loving being asked out for one of their mother's special meals.

"Sarah knows I like my potatoes baked," Ethan said smiling at his fiancé, who didn't do more than shrug a shoulder.

"Isaac?"

"Scalloped potatoes loaded with cream, butter and baked slow in the oven so there's a crisp edge to dig out of the pan."

Brides with Grit

Everyone laughed, then took another bite of his mother's mashed potatoes. Jacob had to agree that mashed was his favorite too, and hoped that Rania would ask his mother how to make them.

"So when's your wedding, Sarah?" Hilda asked, trying to pull his sister into a conversation.

"I'm not sure…" Sarah put her fork on her plate and looked down at her lap.

"Saturday, June 14th, Flag Day," Ethan interrupted Sarah. "I wanted it the first weekend in May but Sarah thought the hotel my parents are building should be done first. My parents and I agreed because the wedding will make a grand opening for the hotel, and a nice place for the reception." The Freemans' plan was for Ethan and Sarah to live in the new Clear Creek hotel and manage it once they were married.

Both Sarah and Cate's mouths gaped open like it was news to both of them. After looking at her daughter's flushed face, Cate tried to soothe over the awkward situation. "I'll talk to your parents first, Ethan, before we announce the date."

"Well the hotel is almost finished, so we need to get the grand opening set, move in and start running it."

"Ethan," Cate evenly said, turning to look him straight in the eye, "the wedding doesn't have to coincide with the hotel's opening." Jacob could see his mother's right eyebrow go up and her left eye narrow when she responded to Ethan. She was a patient woman—unless she felt her children were being threatened—and her patience was starting to wear thin on the subject of her daughter's wedding. The Freemans were a wonderful family and pillars of the community, but Cate was concerned that Ethan wasn't the best match for Sarah. He was nine years older than her, but the real problem was there was absolutely

29

no spark between them, let alone affection or two–sided conversations.

"In Sweden, you don't worry about getting married right away." Everyone turned to Hilda. "You announce in church three Sundays in a row that you're going to be betrothed, exchange gifts, and move in together. You can have the wedding ceremony sometime in the future, and many wait until the woman is pregnant."

"But you don't get to wear the bride's crown if that's the case," Rania had added without thinking who else was at the table.

Sarah asked, "What's the bride's crown? Do Swedish brides wear it instead of a veil?"

Rania's face was red, but she answered Sarah's question, "Nowadays brides get to wear the church's bridal crown if they are…untouched. It's the church's way to try to get the couple to marry before living together."

"Well, I'm glad we're in America now," Hilda piped in. "When the right man comes along, I'm just going to get married. I won't fuss with a fancy dress, veil or crown."

Jacob laughed with the others at the table. There was such a difference in personality between the twins, but Rania was still the one he preferred, and he couldn't wait to get to know her better.

Conversation changed to other neighbors who the Hamners had yet to meet. "Who lives between our place and yours? The place looks abandoned with no smoke in the chimney," stated Dagmar.

"It's our brother Noah's place," Adam spoke up, "and I'm worried that someone's going to jump his claim pretty soon if he doesn't come home. I was in Ellsworth yesterday and the county

Brides with Grit

land agent told me there's one guy in particular who's been giving him heck for not signing over the claim to him."

"Why isn't your brother on his place? A person has to reside on the land to prove up and own it, don't they?" asked Dagmar.

"Noah met a special girl when he went to Illinois and lived with our grandparents for a while. He and Victoria wrote regularly after he moved back here to build a home for her. When Noah went to get his bride, he found out she had already married someone else. Since then, he's been wandering around working odd jobs instead of coming home."

"Well, after meeting Victoria when we visited our grandparents last year, I'm sure Noah scared Victoria when he wrote that he built her a sod house. That's not quite what a banker's daughter is used to," Sarah injected.

"Did he get around to building any outbuildings on the place?" Rania could almost see Hilda's mind churning when she asked the question.

"Besides the soddie, he built a small barn and chicken house. He planned to add on to the barn at a later time. Some fences are up, but there's more work that needs to be done on the place. It's one hundred sixty acres, with some flat, tillable ground besides a sloping section he planned to use for pasture. It also has the creek running through it, so the water rights are important for those below him, too."

"How would a person take over the homestead?" Hilda asked next.

"Unfortunately, he only paid the $10 temporary file fee, so someone could come in and buy it. Don't know all the particulars though."

Rania Ropes a Rancher

"Well I have talked to the agent, and I can buy land at $1.25 an acre."

"You have that kind of money?" Sarah asked in surprise.

All three Swedish siblings smiled in unison and Dagmar piped up, "Hilda and her gelding Nutcracker enter every horse race she can find, and she usually wins the prize money."

"But she's a woman…" Sarah continued.

"So?" Hilda shot back across the table at Sarah. "I just tuck my hair under my hat, join the racers at the starting point, and leave all the men in Nutcracker's dust." Hilda beamed a wide smile to everyone around the table.

"You know, if you're worried a stranger might take over Noah's place, how about I buy it? My folks would be neighbors on one side, and your family on the other. It sounds like a perfect, safe place to breed and train my horses."

"And Hilda wouldn't mind roughing it in a sod house," Dagmar teased his sister.

"What do you think? Should we let Noah's homestead go to Hilda?" Adam looked at Jacob and his mother for their opinion.

Jacob smiled, thinking of what Noah would say when he finally came home and found this spunky Swedish woman living in his home. Actually this might be exactly what Noah needed to get his life back on track.

"Can we go see the place tomorrow?" Hilda asked Jacob.

"Sure. How about I meet you over there in the morning, say around ten o'clock?"

32

Brides with Grit

"I have a better idea," his mother gently intervened. "Besides stopping at Noah's place, I've love to go see Dagmar's new bachelor home. We've never been invited while the Elisions were in residence. I think Dagmar might need a woman's opinion on what to use and set aside."

Sarah grinned with the idea. "We can pack a picnic lunch, and we four women can give him some advice while we dine there."

"Oh, I don't know..." Dagmar started to protest.

"You don't know what you're getting into, living in a big house by yourself, Dag, so you best take our advice," Hilda quickly cut him off.

"Rania, we'll pick you up in the wagon tomorrow so you don't have to ride over." Jacob gave a silent nod of thanks to his mother for her statement. He was still worried about Rania after her tumble.

Rania Ropes a Rancher

CHAPTER 3

"Oh my…"

Jacob was getting tired of the women saying that phrase as they walked through the Bar E Ranch house. Yes, the two–story sandstone home was huge, and the furnishings were elegant, but their comments as they walked through the house were getting old, and he was getting hungry for the chicken dinner his mother had packed.

Actually it was Hilda doing most of the talking, and picking up almost every fancy crystal glass that caught her eye. His mother and sister had seen fine furnishings before, but the twins seemed to be completely out of their element. Rania just stared, acting like she'd love to touch things, but was too afraid to do so. From the comments between the twins, it sounded like most of their lives had been spent on the trails or in a crude shack on the ranch where they had worked.

"Did they ship all these things from back East? How many are in the Elison family and what do they do in Boston?" The questions kept coming from Hilda faster than Dagmar could answer them.

"Besides Mr. and Mrs. Elison, there are the two sons I mentioned, plus a daughter…I think her name is Cora."

"I don't think Mrs. Elison or Cora has ever been here, have they?" Sarah asked her mother who confirmed no with a shake of her head.

Dagmar's cockiness of living in this grand house was rapidly turning into the reality of him being in charge of the contents. Delicate china and crystal were on display in glass cases in the dining room. Polished carved–leg chairs and a settee covered in a gold velvet fabric gave the parlor a very formal look, especially with the brocade wallpaper and maroon velvet drapes. The downstairs bedroom, plus the four upstairs, featured elaborate bedroom furniture; large, thick area rugs; luxurious linens; with matching pitchers, basins and commodes on the wash stands.

"And you're going to live here by yourself, Dag?" Hilda asked as she wiped a finger over the massive office desk in the den and lifted her finger to show him the dust on the tip of it.

"Yes, I'm supposed to. The Elison family will visit now and then, but Mr. Elison said it was better for the house to be lived in than left empty." Dagmar turned his hat around and around in his fidgeting hands as he spoke. "Believe me, I'll have you over to dust and polish the brass candlesticks when I get a telegram saying they're on their way."

Luckily Jacob's mother took over to calm Dagmar's panic attack. "Dagmar, after lunch we'll move things around a bit so you'll feel comfortable living in the downstairs bedroom and kitchen."

These two rooms had more space than the sod house that they had first toured at Noah's homestead, plus so much more sunlight streaming through the house. Hilda was excited about the home

36

Brides with Grit

and buildings, though, and was anxious to go into Ellsworth to put the land in her name. Jacob could tell she liked the house they were touring now, but would be just as comfortable in a sod home with a dirt floor. The soddie, though, was very dark when you compare it to the light brought in by the grand windows in this house.

Rania seemed recovered from her fall, but Jacob's mind flashed back to her body sprawled on the ground whenever he glanced at her bruised forehead. Would he ever get over the panic of seeing Rania's face covered with blood? She had been in his thoughts day and night since he found her.

***

"Is that the whole flock?" Hilda asked with a chuckle. After lunch they toured the Bar E barn and outbuildings and now stood in a small nearby pasture. Two half–grown lambs curiously looked at the lineup of people in their territory from behind a huge, white Pyrenees guard dog.

"The entire flock was sold, but they couldn't get the final two sheep away from the dog," Dagmar told her. "Mr. Elison said I could shoot the last sheep for meat. He said to shoot the dog, too. No one can get near him or the sheep."

"Are you sure the dog isn't eating a sheep a day?" Hilda gasped the question. "He's gigantic, and weighs more than you do!"

Rania walked away from her family about twenty feet and stopped to see what the dog would do. The dog eyed her, then the group, back at his charges and back to her. After a few minutes, Rania slowly walked closer to the animals.

"Rania…watch him. No one's been able to get close to the dog or the sheep without him growling and showing his teeth," Dagmar warned.

"Do you know his name?"

"One of ranch hands said 'King', named for this variety of dog that was bred to watch over royalty."

"So what and how are you feeding him, if he won't leave his flock?"

"I guess he hunts rabbits and such when he feels the flock is safe. There are also two cattle dogs here, so I assume he lets them stand watch at times. I suppose I should to toss him scraps now and then."

"Come here, King. It's okay," Rania softly spoke when she was within ten feet of the dog. After a moment's hesitation, the dog lowered his head and ambled toward her like he was finally relaxed and free of his duty. The sheep followed closely behind and then surrounded Rania when the dog lay at Rania's feet. Rania leaned over, scratching the dog's head, which brought out a happy groan from the animal.

"So now what, are you part of his flock?" Dagmar asked in frustration, probably after all the trouble he had heard about between the ranch hands, dog and sheep. "A good sheep guard dog doesn't mingle with people, nor should they be treated as pets." But when Rania started walking back to her family, the three animals followed her—with the dog guarding in front of course.

The big dog gave Rania the first feeling of security she had enjoyed since leaving Texas. She wondered if the dog would leave the Bar E, if it could bring his flock with him. "Dagmar, would it be okay if the group moved with me to our parents' ranch?"

Brides with Grit

"Why would you want to bother?"

"When you and Hilda move to your new homes, I'll be there by myself until our parents come back." Then she quickly added, "I'm sure Mother would like to start a flock for fleece and meat. She and our grandmothers used to card and spin wool into yarn."

She wondered if Jacob noticed her quick afterthought to cover up her insecurity. She so hoped that Dagmar and King would cooperate with her request.

"I think that's a fine idea," Cate responded to Rania's question before Dagmar had a chance to say anything. "We'll herd them home for you when we leave this afternoon, and Jacob will check on them every day to be sure they get settled in." Rania felt her cheeks blush when Jacob gave a questioning look to his mother. But it seems like her sons never questioned her courteous commands.

***

The next week, as Dagmar and Hilda grew more excited about having their own homes; Jacob thought Rania seemed to withdraw. She was going to be alone in the house, left to clean and sort through the past owner's belongings herself.

The women set up Dagmar's bachelor rooms in the Bar E house first. Jacob thought they talked about every item they moved—and where to move them—in that big house for the next two days.

Hilda bought Noah's place and took an inventory of his sparse household things. Jacob packed Noah's personal belongings and brought them over to the family home. Hilda made a list of staples and items she wanted to buy and the women took the wagon to town for a shopping spree. For a woman who always dressed in

39

men's trousers, Jacob couldn't believe that frilly curtains were the top priority on Hilda's list.

As promised, Jacob rode over every day to check the "flock" even though he had plenty to do on his own ranch. The two ranch houses were only a mile apart so it was easy to take a break and visit Rania. His mother seemed attuned with Rania's insecurities and drove over at different times with produce from her garden, or eggs and milk. Jacob realized that Rania had to find her own way of being comfortable in her new life, though. He'd have to practice his patience until he could ask to be included in it.

CHAPTER 4

"Hello the house and Rania!"

"What are you doing over here with a draft horse?" Rania asked as she strolled out of the house while flipping the drying towel on top of her shoulder. Rania had been washing dishes when she heard the harness clattering outside. Jacob was riding the draft bareback, sitting behind the work collar and harness the horse was wearing.

"Come over to work your garden plot. There's a single plow in the barn so I just needed to bring the right horse for the job. I assume you want the garden in the same spot Sam had it?"

"And what am I going to plant in this garden?"

"Grow whatever your family would like to eat this winter. You said there were some seeds in jars in the cellar, and of course Ma sent seeds over for you too," Jacob replied as he pulled a small paper–wrapped package out of his left boot. "I'll hitch the horse to the plow and meet you in the garden."

"Are you going to work Hilda's garden too?" Rania couldn't help asking.

Rania Ropes a Rancher

"I've already been there this morning and worked her ground. Thought I'd do yours second so I can help you plant and get rewarded with dinner."

Rania couldn't help but smile back at the flash of dimples in the man's cheeks. If she didn't watch it, she could fall in love with Jacob. But even if he showed interest in her, how would that work—if she had another man's baby growing inside her?

***

"What's your favorite kind of pickle?" Jacob was digging holes with the hoe while Rania trailing behind, dropping cucumber seeds in the holes, before kicking a bit of soil over the seeds and stepping on the spot to cover them.

"Dill," answered Rania. She was getting used to his question game, so knew to answer whatever came to her mind first.

"Well mine is 'Bread and Butter' so be sure to preserve some jars of that for me, too, when you harvest all these cucumbers." They had planted cucumbers, corn, beans and squash seeds so far this morning. The leftover potatoes from last winter that were left in the cellar had been brought upstairs already, cut into eye pieces, and lay drying out in the sun. Jacob said he'd help plant them after dinner, hinting he really meant he wanted to share a meal with her.

Luckily Rania had some bread, butter and eggs left over from Cate's visit the day before. It seemed like Jacob had a knack for arriving around the noon meal, so she needed to start planning ahead for company meals. It was a routine she really enjoyed and looked forward to each day. *I wish it could be like this every day. Jacob would be a loving husband and a protective father.*

Jacob entered the house and washed on the back porch. Then before she had time to clear the table, Jacob started to set things

Brides with Grit

aside for her. Sam's writing box, which he remembered from visiting the man, was on the table.

"Rania, have you opened this box yet?"

"No, I haven't found a key. I hear things inside when I shake the box so I wish I could open it. There might be letters that need to be answered or sent on to his family."

"It might hold important papers like the deed to this homestead, too." Jacob dug his pen knife out of his pocket and opened a small blade. Who knows where the key might be, so he'd pry it open. "If I can't get the lock opened with my knife, I'll check the tool shed for something else to use."

***

After lunch Jacob opened the writing box, spread the contents out on the kitchen table and they began sorting and reading the papers.

"Jacob, there's a stack of letters from a Millie Donovan from Chicago. The postmarks start last fall and...this last one is dated March. What about his mail since Sam passed?"

"The postmaster knew he died, so I assume he sent letters back to the senders."

Rania opened the newest letter to read first. After a quick scan, she started over, telling Jacob the highlights of the contents. "Oh, Jacob, this letter from Millie says her sister in Missouri is expecting a baby...so she's leaving Chicago now—which would have been in March—and she will be with her sister until early May when she, Millie, will travel on to Kansas to meet Sam. She looks forward to becoming his bride!"

Rania Ropes a Rancher

After that discovery, they read the other letters starting from the beginning, learning that Millie and Sam met through a mail–order bride advertisement. Apparently Sam had asked her to move to Kansas, because they read Millie's acceptance in one of the letters.

"There's also an envelope with a woman's wedding ring in it," Rania said as she handed the letter over to Jacob.

Jacob took out the simple gold band, holding it between his thumb and finger, secretly wondering what it would look like on Rania's ring finger. "Looks like Sam was ready for the ceremony. I wonder if the preacher in town knew about this. And how do we get word to the unsuspecting woman that she needs to stay at her sister's?"

"I wonder if Sam sent a picture of himself to her. There was no picture of Millie in any letter." Rania got out of her seat, and walked into the bedroom, calling back over her shoulder, "I've packed all his personal things in a box that I thought we should send to his family. There are photos in the box, so maybe Millie's picture is in it."

Minutes later Rania and Jacob had four individual photos of women laid out on the table. "These could be family members, or Millie, or other women he's corresponded with in the past," pondered Rania.

"They are all fairly young women; no names written on the back of the photos. Did Millie describe her features in any of the letters?"

"No," confessed Rania. "It was more 'by my photo you'll recognize me at the train station' instead of her telling him her hair or eye coloring. No mention of what color of hat or dress she'd be wearing either."

44

Brides with Grit

"Because Millie didn't mention her sister's name or town, we have no way of contacting Millie. It sounds like she'll be arriving soon, too. I suppose we should give these letters and the photos to Adam, and he can meet the train each day and try to intercept her. I hope she has funds to travel back to her sister, because there's no reason for her to stay here."

***

"What color portrayed your childhood?" Jacob asked Rania as they watched King herd the two sheep back into the pasture after coming up to drink in the water tank by the barn.

He let that sink into her mind and then continued. "What's your childhood color?" Jacob asked again. He glanced at Rania, but she seemed deep in thought, either about his question, or something else on her mind.

Jacob responded to his own question since Rania didn't answer, "I'd say mine was 'Union Blue'. We lived in Illinois just as the War Between the States exploded with the attack on Fort Sumter in South Carolina in 1861. When we heard the news a few days later, Pa said we were heading west if the war wasn't settled soon. When battles continued into the next year, our farm was sold and we were on the road by early spring. My grandparents were Quakers, and instilled in Pa that fighting and slavery were wrong. He did not want his sons drawn into the battles in the war."

Rania looked at him. "Well I don't blame him. I wouldn't want my sons in a war either. How old were you?"

"I was fourteen and wanted to get in on the fighting so bad…that's all I talked about. It seemed so exciting and patriotic. I wanted to be wearing Union Blue and carry Pa's old Springfield Model 1855 rifle musket.

45

"Adam was a year older than me and more into the rights and wrongs of the states leaving the Union. You can guess why he's a marshal now."

Jacob looked her way to see if she'd comment with a nod or word, but now her eyes were looking toward the horizon, so Jacob just kept talking. "Adam still has that same need to correct the wrongs that happen in society. Everything is pretty much right or wrong to Clear Creek's marshal. He sees things in black and white, no gray areas to his way of thinking at all.

"My younger brother, Noah, just wanted to tag along with the two of us. He's more of a happy–go–lucky guy, but very loyal to his family and friends.

"My parents were afraid we'd all three end up fighting in the war, so they decided to put some distance between us and the recruiting people.

"I was upset with moving and losing out on my dream of being a Union soldier, but now I'm glad I didn't participate in the battles. The war's end brought a whole lot of soldiers west, many disabled, trying to run from their nightmares, having no family or home left, especially if they came from the Confederate states that were burned and ravaged. I sometimes feel guilty when men mock me for staying out of the war, but I sleep easier at night because of my Quaker–minded father's decision."

Jacob fell silent, but still thinking back to moving. Kansas had obtained statehood the year before, but the eastern part of the state was fighting with Missouri about slavery issues, so his family kept going west until they settled near a trading ranch.

"But we still ended up with soldiers around us a few years later when the Indians became hostile with all the settlers moving in on their land. That's how Fort Harker got started and my wish of wearing Union Blue flared up again. I was a seventeen–year–old, ready to ride into battle…although it was on the prairie instead of the Civil War battlefield. Pa took us boys over to the fort when a struggling unit was bringing wounded soldiers back from a skirmish. I really think that day set the destiny of career choices for all of us. Adam wanted to go into law enforcement; I wanted to run a ranch to supply the army with food and livestock, and Noah decided he wanted to go back to Illinois."

Jacob fell silent, thinking how the Civil War changed all their lives.

"Falun Red." Jacob glanced sideways at Rania when she spoke.

"It's a deep red color that most homes in Sweden are painted. The paint is made of water, rye flour, linseed oil and the tailings from the copper mines of Falun.

"The idyllic place every Swedish woman wanted was a pretty, red cottage, bordered with flowers, and a field of potatoes beside it." *But the color from the mine slimes came with a price.*

Jacob leaned against the board fence, listening to Rania as she opened up about her childhood.

"My father worked in the depths of a copper mine and came home every night black from soot, and stank from sweat and rock. He'd spend his day in the dark heat, digging and breaking out the ore, and setting it on fire to break up overnight. Next morning, they'd put out the fires, and start over again. Most nights he spent drinking to put out the thirst and memories. Most miners were drunks."

Rania sighed, but continued after a moment. "Momma had a cousin from a nearby parish who was leaving for America to work on a Texas ranch. The rancher had ties with our area and, for years, had been paying ship passage for families who would work at his ranch.

"Momma knew Leif and Dagmar would be joining our father in the mines soon, just as several generations before them had done. That's all our men knew to do, and they would die young, too."

Rania stopped talking but now Jacob wanted to know more, so he asked, "So your parents decided to move to America?"

She gave a slight laugh when he asked. "I was only nine at the time, but I remember my very drunk father being coerced onto the ship, and he was very belligerent for at least a week at sea." Her eyes looked like she was back on the ocean staring at the waves of water instead of grass. "But weeks later we had a new, sober father, who had a better outlook on life when we reached America's shore. My mother's decision to move to Texas saved my father and our family."

He asked a question that had been on his mind since he met her.

"You have the Texas drawl down pretty good, but you still have a little Swedish lilt to your voice. Do you still talk Swedish at home?"

"We do, even though we've been in Texas for fourteen years. Most of the ranch workers came from Sweden, so it's a given. But we children went to school so learned English there."

"So you still want a Falun Red home someday?"

Rania turned and looked Jacob in the eye. "Oh, don't know. It just reminds me of home, you know?"

Brides with Grit

Jacob opened the gate by the barn, and said, "Let's walk over to the creek and check on the horses. Looks like your stallion Thor and his ladies are enjoying the shade of the few trees along the banks." After Rania walked through, Jacob closed the gate behind them. He held out his big hand until she finally clasped it in hers. Jacob gave it a squeeze and started walking toward the creek.

"Sunrise or sunset?"

"Sunrise," Rania answered as she stared at the far horizon.

"Why? Give me an example," prompted Jacob.

"It may have been cold to get out of my bedroll before dawn on the trail, but seeing the very first hint of light on the eastern sky was always my favorite time of day.

"It was Hilda's and my task to get the remuda in before first light. The horses were fresh and it was always fun to see the horses kick up their heels for the heck of it. Sometimes, depending on the horse the rider picked for the day, we'd have a bronco ride or two to watch. It didn't last long, and the riders knew to expect it, so they rarely got dumped off the horses.

"Momma served breakfast by campfire light when just a thin strip of yellow light was starting to show behind her. By the time we got the chuck and supply wagons loaded up, we'd have a brilliant show of morning color as we took off for the day."

They continued walking across the pasture, looking at the sky, deep in their own thoughts.

"I think I'm going to say sunset. Most evenings I stand in the middle of the yard when the sun is going down. I look toward the barn where multi–colored waves, be they bright or gray, fill the western horizon behind it, and I think about what I've accomplished out under the big sky since the last sunset. Then I

49

can turn around, to view the outline of the house in the darkening eastern sky, and see a lamp lit in the house that's waiting for me to come home. Right now it's my mother and sister waiting for me, but I think they will both move out eventually."

"Then the house will be dark and there will be no one to greet you," Rania sadly responded.

Jacob gave Rania's hand another squeeze. "I hope to have my own wife and children lighting the lamp and waiting to welcome me home soon."

Rania looked up when Jacob didn't release her hand. His eyes held a hint of sparkle as he stared at her lips, and his mouth was turned up in a half grin.

Her breath hitched with the feeling that Jacob knew who he wanted waiting for him at night—but did she deserve to be the one?

She wondered what it would be like to be kissed by Jacob. The kisses by her attacker were sweet at first, but then turned forceful and punishing. Could she ever be kissed by someone like Jacob and not have those terrible memories surface?

The horse herd lifted their heads from grazing when they heard her and Jacob. Thor snorted and the herd moved closer to him. Rania looked over the two mares that were about to foal. She loved baby animals and couldn't wait to welcome the new arrivals to the herd.

Rania rubbed her abdomen, wondering if she'd be welcoming a baby soon. Her mind said it was true, but her heart hadn't accepted it yet. She knew her family would have no problem with an addition to the family, but Rania was afraid that it wouldn't fit well with Jacob's plans for the future.

50

Brides with Grit

"Everything looks all right out here, Jacob, so we can go back to the house. I'm sure you have things to do at your ranch instead of spending time here." Rania glanced at Jacob when she made the announcement and dropped his hand to turn around. He looked puzzled, but didn't say anything.

The time for telling Jacob about her pregnancy was advancing rapidly whether she was ready or not. But she'd wait a few more days before breaking the news to him. She wanted more walks and talks before he left her for good after hearing her news.

Rania Ropes a Rancher

CHAPTER 5

Jacob chose sunset to ride over to the Bar E Ranch to talk to Dagmar. Hopefully Dagmar would be riding in from the range rather than staying out overnight. It was always a guess as to who was outriding the herd, but Jacob knew Dagmar took turns with the four hands who lived in the bunkhouse and worked on the ranch.

He was nervous to talk to the youngest Hamner, but Jacob didn't have an option if he was going to do it right. His father always said the right way was always the best way to approach everything—whether working with a green horse, or maybe even a certain skittish woman he'd taken a shine to. Jacob needed to ask a male Hamner for the right to court Rania, and because her father wasn't here to ask him, Dagmar would be the one to hopefully give his blessing.

"Hey, Jacob! Tie up your horse and come into the house," called Dagmar. Jacob rode into the yard just as Dagmar was knocking his boots off at the door.

Jacob tied Duncan's reins to the front hitching post and walked up the porch steps, his spurs jingling with each step.

Rania Ropes a Rancher

"Oh, please take off your boots Jacob, before you enter the house."

"Why?" Jacob teased, "Don't you want to clean house, Dagmar?"

"You got that right. I still don't feel comfortable living in this huge house by myself. Plus I'm still tip–toeing whenever I go near a fancy crystal thing, so you know I'm walking on the balls of my feet most of the time."

Jacob laughed out loud at Dagmar's blushing face and confession. Here's this huge man, scared to death of some little glass objects. "Yes, this house is full of fancy stuff so I'm sure your boots aren't touching those nice carpets. I assume you stay in the two rooms that the women fixed up for you?"

"Yes, I'm still worried about the rest of the house, so I make a round through all the rooms before I go to bed, otherwise I'd never get any shuteye," Dagmar sighed.

"Okay, then let's just sit on the porch chairs to talk, then, so I don't have to take off my boots. How are things going otherwise on the ranch?" Jacob asked to get Dagmar's mind off the fancy furnishings he was living among.

"I feel comfortable outside. The ranch is ten sections, so we have over six thousand acres for the herd to graze on. The hands take turns staying with the herd at all times. Now and then we find a few cattle marked with other brands than the Bar E, but we'll get them sorted out this fall when we round up the herd and brand the calves."

"How's your help?"

"Mr. Elison fired two hands, but I hired replacements who came around the first week. They are young boys, but they know

Brides with Grit

how to ride and rope so they will work out—and are loyal to the Bar E brand. There's an older man, Reuben Shepard living in the bunkhouse, who cooks and washes for the hands, I usually eat with them so I don't have to dirty a dish in the house. He's a good father figure for the young hands, so I'm glad there's someone we can all lean on when we need him."

"Your sisters been around much?" Jacob was curious if Rania had been out riding by herself again.

"No, I think they are both cleaning houses, but I wish they'd show up with some sweets now and then. Don't tell them, I do miss their chatter too. You get used to women talking all the time, and then it gets real quiet when they aren't in the house anymore."

"So Dagmar, since you're the only Hamner man living here at the moment, I assume you're in charge of your sisters' care?"

Dagmar snorted, "Are you kidding me? They'd thump both of our heads if they heard your question. Why do you ask for heaven's sake?"

Jacob straightened up and looked into Dagmar's eyes. "I want to ask your permission to court Rania." *There. He said it.*

Dagmar stared at him a moment as in shock. "Why?"

"Because I like her," Jacob said in exasperation, wondering why Dagmar would ask such a simple, but stupid, question.

"Have you kissed her? Do I need to do something about her honor?"

"Dagmar, no I haven't kissed her yet—but I'd like to. And honestly I'm interested in asking for her hand in marriage eventually. Rania's been awfully quiet compared to last year when we met, so I've been going slowly with my attentions toward her."

55

Dagmar rubbed a socked foot against the porch floor. "Something has been bothering Rania, but she hasn't said anything to me or Hilda. She got downright spooky on the trail, but has settled down here in Kansas," Dagmar agreed. "I think you'd be good for Rania, so please begin courting—and good luck."

Jacob's heart swelled in his chest as he thought of kissing Rania, and then his head caused it to skip a beat. "Uh, got any suggestions on how to gain her confidence?"

"Jacob, I'm a man and clueless, so you best ask another female…"

***

"Hey, Ma. Enjoying the evening air?" His parents had enjoyed sitting on the porch swing at the end of the day when the weather was nice. After his father died of cancer, his mother continued the ritual. Jacob and his siblings left her alone at first, often hearing her talk to their father like he was still alive. She shared her worries, telling his ghost what was going on around the ranch, and with their children. Eventually he and his siblings took turns sitting in the porch swing to give her company. His ma had survived her grief and looked forward to life again.

"Come sit down and enjoy the spring air with me. Where'd you go this evening?" She scooted over to one side of the swing, barely stopping the motion with her foot until Jacob sat down and his foot took over the rhythm she had started.

Jacob took a breath before making his announcement, hoping his mother would like it. "I went over to see Dagmar and asked his permission to court Rania."

Brides with Grit

Back and forth, back and forth…Jacob kept the swing moving but became worried when his mother wasn't answering immediately.

"She's a fine match for you Jacob, but there are issues you'll have to discuss before marriage."

Jacob was surprised by her answer. "Like what?"

"It's a lifetime commitment, and you've heard the vows. You have to give and take, accept the other person as they are—and what they may become decades later—and be ready for what life throws at you."

Jacob took his mother's hand between his. "Don't you think I'm ready for marriage? I expected you to jump for joy at my choice of wife."

His mother squeezed his hand and smiled at him. "Yes, I think you're ready. Rania will make a fine wife, but you're going to have to accept her as she is first."

"You're talking in riddles, Ma."

"Tell her what's in your heart and ask her to be honest with you. I think it will work out."

"Okay, well I didn't think this conversation would turn so serious. I meant to ask you what I should do to win her over. Any gift ideas?"

"Oh where shall I start?" she beamed, back to her usual self. "You ask her questions all the time. What's her favorite color, flower, any hobbies she'd like to try? *And don't buy her a dust pan for goodness sake.* Make it a personal item for her to enjoy, not related to housework.

Rania Ropes a Rancher

"Your father only made that mistake once before I shed tears—and then told him off." She chuckled with a memory. Jacob was almost afraid to ask what the item was, just couldn't resist.

"What did Pa give you?"

"He gave me a mouse trap for my first birthday after we were married. Not a fancy pin or book, but a trap to catch the filthy mice that were taking over the house. The poor man thought he was helping me, but it was so disappointing to open up the little box and see a trap. A cat with a pretty ribbon around its neck would have better, but no, it was a trap I had to bait, hear its deadly snap, take the dead mouse outside to dispose of it, set the trap again…" Jacob's hands were being squeezed hard with his mother's memories so he shook her hands off.

"Okay, okay. I won't ever do that then. What are some ideas for gifts?"

She folded her arms, and then tapped a finger against her chin. "The twins were talking about the tradition of gifts when a couple was going to get married in Sweden. Three Sundays it was announced in church and gifts to go with it. You don't have to do any announcing in church here, but a gift each week is a nice idea, and I think she'd appreciate the sentiment."

"Wasn't that when the couple became betrothed?"

"Yes." His mother stared him in the eye like she was thinking the same thing. Then she continued, "What's her favorite flower?"

"Ah, I get points for asking her that question already. Her favorite flower in Sweden was the twin flower, only an inch tall that had two fragrant pink flowers per stem, but only grows in the shaded forests. When I asked what her favorite American flower was, Rania said she loved the scent of the lilac bushes that

58

Brides with Grit

bloomed around our house the first time she came here in early May."

"You have some good clues to start with then. Instead of giving her flowers, give her a pretty glass vase, *and then* take her for a walk and pick flowers *with her* to fill the vase." He could do that since they were already taking walks and the prairie was starting to sprout wildflowers.

"Another idea…a woman always feels feminine when given scented water, especially if you comment you like the scent of it on her skin or hair. You probably haven't noticed it on the shelf in the general store but it comes in variety of scents like rose, and lilac…"

"That's two gifts. What shall I do for the third?"

His mother grinned at him, "You figure out yourself what the final gift should be to win her heart."

***

Jacob rode into town early the next morning and was waiting at Taylor's General Store when they opened their doors. The lilac water was easy to find, but then he had to make a choice on which vase to pick. He wracked his brain; trying to think what style of vase Rania liked the most when they had been in the Elison house that first visit. He finally told Mrs. Taylor who the gift was for, and she immediately picked up the vase that she said Rania had looked at once. He carefully packed the paper–wrapped gifts in his saddle bag, rode to Rania's, and now stood on her porch with the first gift behind his back.

Jacob knocked on the front door—and there was no answer. But then King "woofed" behind him, almost causing Jacob to drop the present as he spun around to face the dog, and of course Rania.

59

"Good morning, Jacob," Rania smiled, trying to hide her amusement at his sudden jump when she and King surprised him.

"Hello, Rania. Nice to see you." Jacob rocked back and forth on his boot heels, not quite sure if Rania saw the package he held behind his back, and what he should do next.

"Uh, this is for you, Rania." Jacob blushed, not believing how tongue–tied he felt all of a sudden. And then realized he hadn't handed her the present yet, so thrust it at her.

Rania took the package, now blushing too. "Should I open it now?"

"Yes, please. But be careful, it's…maybe you should open it on the kitchen table." Jacob gestured to the front porch, turned the door handle and gestured again for Rania to enter first.

Rania walked in, and glanced back at Jacob as he followed her into the kitchen. He sat down in a chair, folded his hands on the table, and gripped them tightly as she turned the brown paper–wrapped package around and around in her hands.

"What is it?" Rania teased as she probed the paper and watched Jacob grit his teeth while he tried to smile.

She slowly, and carefully, turned the item in one hand and pulled the paper off an inch at a time with the other hand. Jacob released his held breath in relief as Rania gasped and smiled at the vase she held in her hand. "This is beautiful, Jacob. Is this really for me?"

"Do you like it?" Jacob was so happy with her surprised explanation; he felt seven feet tall instead of six. He rose, and took her hand, "How about we take a walk and find some pretty flowers to put in your new vase?"

60

Brides with Grit

When Jacob got to the front door, he reached for his hat that he usually put on the wall peg when he came into her house, then felt his face flush when he realized his hat was still on his head. He hadn't taken off his hat when he came in. Good grief. He needed to calm down, or he'd never be able to ask to court her.

The sky was blue, the wind calm and Jacob had never seen so many wildflowers in his life now that his world was looking rosy. Rania flitted from one bunch of flowers to the next, barely containing her excitement at filling her new vase with fresh flowers. Jacob felt like a hero, following Rania around with his pocket knife, cutting the stems she pointed at, and felt like a prince when he handed the cut flower to her outstretched hand. Her arm was full of so many flowers when they walked back to the house that he wished he could have bought a crystal bucket to hold the bouquet instead of a little vase.

"I think I picked enough flowers for several arrangements. I'll put the best stems in your pretty vase to view from the kitchen table, and put the rest in a pitcher to set on my bedroom dresser." Rania looked so happy right now that Jacob knew it was time for his big announcement. But first, he'd try for a kiss—after she got her flowers arranged like she wanted them.

When Rania walked back from the bedroom Jacob stood and took her hands. "Like your gift?" He returned her big smile and changed his hands to hold her waist. "Maybe enough to give me a little thank–you kiss?" Jacob teased.

He felt Rania tense up a moment, but then relax. "I like that you're tall, Rania. I can look you straight in the eye instead of having to bend down. And it's so handy to kiss you, too." Jacob softly touched Rania's lips for a second, and then backed off to look in her eyes. *Why were they squeezed shut?* Then Rania opened her eyes and leaned up and touched her lips to his, making him forget his worry.

Jacob felt elated as Rania's arms wrapped around his shoulders, pulling him against her chest. This was what he wanted, a passionate woman he could share his life with. The kiss felt so right between them and he wanted to continue savoring her lips forever, but he forced himself to stop and pull Rania away at arm's length. It was time to talk.

"Rania, I've already talked to Dagmar and asked his permission." Rania looked confused, so Jacob took a deep breath and smiled to calm her worried face. "I think you're very special and I have a question to ask you." Jacob took another breath before continuing, "I'd like to court you in hopes that you'd agree to become my wife."

Her shocked look, then crumbling face was not what he expected at all. "Rania? What's wrong?" Rania was starting to hyperventilate until she got herself under control.

"I...I have to tell you something, Jacob. I'm honored that you asked me but..."

"But what?" Jacob asked warily as the hairs on the back of his neck stood up. This wasn't the reaction he thought he'd get from Rania.

"I think I'm pregnant."

Jacob stepped back like she had just slapped him. "What did you just say?"

Rania looked like she could faint, but his arms weren't about to catch her.

62

Brides with Grit

She wouldn't look at him when she said again, "I'm pregnant."

Jacob's shocked silence caused Rania to lift her eyes to meet his. Tears streamed down her face but she didn't lift a hand to wipe them away, and neither did he.

Jacob spun on his heel and stormed out the door, forgetting he had hung his hat on the peg by the door this time.

"Jacob, please let me explain…" Rania called after him, but Jacob didn't stop his rapid descent from the porch.

Rania Ropes a Rancher

CHAPTER 6

Blind fury raced through Jacob as Duncan took him home. It's a wonder the horse didn't throw him for the way he acted and, at the moment, Jacob didn't care. How could Rania be with someone else and lead him on for the past month? When was she seeing the other man? Did they laugh behind his back at his stupid attempt at romancing? Here Jacob thought she was shy and reserved and instead she was seeing two men at once.

No, his mind volleyed back. If she knew she was pregnant, it meant it was someone she'd been with in Texas before moving up to Kansas. He'd been scared to give her a kiss, but she had been with a man in the most intimate way a couple could be. It just made him sick thinking about it.

Duncan skidded to a stop at the house, still jumpy because of Jacob's attitude. Jacob jumped out of the saddle, and then struggled to dig the wrapped package of Lilac Water out of the saddle bag. When the package was free, Jacob threw it so hard against the ground it smashed, spreading the liquid scent into the air. Duncan jerked the reins off the hitching post to trot away and seek shelter in the barn. Jacob leaned over the mess, positive that

Rania Ropes a Rancher

he could never see or smell a lilac flower again without thinking of the news Rania had just thrown in his face.

Jacob heard his mother come up beside him, and pulled away when she touched his shoulder. He couldn't face her with Rania's confession still bouncing through his head.

You have to give and take; accept the other person as they are...be ready for what life will throw at you. Rania will make a fine wife, but you're going to have to accept her as she is first.

His mother's words came back to him and he swung around to face her.

"*You knew.* Why didn't you tell me Rania was pregnant?" Jacob accused his mother.

Cate calmly folded her arms across her chest before answering. "It was not my business to tell you. Did you talk about the circumstances and how it happened?"

Jacob pointed a finger at her and angrily replied, "I'll not marry someone who loves someone else."

"Is that what she said?" Cate asked in disbelief.

"I didn't stick around to get an explanation or ask any questions. She can go back to Texas to marry the man or stick it out on her own here. I won't be a substitute daddy for her brat." Jacob was so steamed he couldn't even say Rania's name out loud.

"Jacob, she was attacked on the trail up here." Jacob turned and looked at his mother, not believing her excuse for Rania. He also took in that his mother had one hand wrapped tightly around her middle and her other hand was slowly rubbing her neck up and down. He'd seen her do that a few times when she was really stressed.

66

Brides with Grit

"I can't believe it wasn't a willing act. She's big and strong enough to punch a man in the gut… or shoot him."

Cate took a deep breath and asked, "What bothers you the most, the thought of a baby on the way or her being with another man?"

His mother's word deflated the anger pulsing through his veins. "I wanted to be her first and only love." Then Jacob blurted out another fear, "And the baby won't look like me."

"Jacob, it was an act of violence against Rania and she didn't love the man. She had no choice when he did it to her."

"There are always choices," he growled.

"Yes and what if *her* choice was to protect someone else? What would you do to protect me, Sarah or Rania?'

"I'd…I'd do anything, until my breath was gone," Jacob confessed, closing his eyes, shuddering with the thought.

"And why would it bother you that the child might not look exactly like you?" His mother continued after a long pause. "Think of your sister Sarah. She has beautiful black hair, so different than you three brown–haired boys. Do you love Sarah less because she isn't an exact copy of you three brothers and your father?"

"No," Jacob agreed. "You have one sister with a similar color hair to Sarah's, and your other sister is a redhead. I know family genetics have a way of sneaking down the generations." Sarah didn't look like their mother, but had differences he had always attributed to their grandparents.

"But she must have had a choice," Jacob picked up his argument again.

67

Rania Ropes a Rancher

"RANIA'S CHOICE WAS TO PROTECT HER FAMILY!" Jacob stared at his mother after her loud, sharp words. She was rubbing her throat harder now.

Her actions caused a childhood memory to flash in Jacob's mind. Their father was away on an errand that day, and a mean, drunk, foul-smelling man had pushed his way into the house. His mother told her young sons to go find the new kittens she thought were in the barn or granary...and not to come back until they found them.

When he and his brothers came back to the house to tell their mother they couldn't find any kittens...she was scrubbing her face in her bedroom wash basin...and then rubbing her hand over and over her throat.

"What if it was Sarah—or me—who had to do something to protect someone we loved? Would you think less of us?" his mother asked in a slight whisper.

That's when his adult mind realized the horror that his six–year–old one could not have comprehended that day long ago in their Illinois house. His mother *chose* to protect Adam, Noah and himself—at her own physical and emotional expense.

Jacob took a step and wrapped his arms tightly around his mother, rubbing her back, realizing what she was trying to tell him. "I'm so, *so* sorry, Ma. Thank you for always protecting us when we were little."

His mother shuddered, and sighed against his chest. "Did Pa know what happened?" Jacob squeezed his eyes shut, thinking of the pain his parents endured because of one dastardly deed that his mother suffered to protect her three young sons.

Brides with Grit

"We never kept secrets from each other, and we rejoiced when we had a healthy baby daughter to love."

"Does Sarah know?"

"It didn't matter to us which man conceived her, so no, we never told her. *She is our daughter, Jacob.* I've never told this to anyone before. I'm only doing so now to make you see that Rania had a choice to make, and it was to protect her family."

"She's the right woman for you, but only if you can fully accept her and the baby together. Marriage is a lifetime commitment."

His mother leaned back in his arms to stare into his eyes. "If you're not sure, then tell Rania and let her move on. There are plenty of men around here who would love to ask Rania's hand in marriage and welcome a baby, too. That baby is growing inside her and she needs to make some crucial decisions for the two of them soon.

"Do you love her, Jacob?"

Jacob immediately wanted to say "yes", but his mother was right that he need to seriously think about this, because it was a lifelong commitment to not only Rania, but also her child on the way.

Then his mother was back to rubbing her throat again. "Please go. I need to be alone for a bit. Sarah should be back from town at any moment, and I need to compose myself. And you need to clean up that pile of glass you left in front of the house."

***

He still smelled the Lilac Water, even after he got a shovel from the barn and buried the shattered glass, the wet paper and the scented top dirt in the bottom of a two–foot hole. Then he realized the water probably splattered on his pants because he threw the bottle so hard on the ground.

After he went back in the house and changed to another pair, he thought it best to rub his boots in the manure in the corral before heading into town. Jacob decided to buy another bottle of the stuff, even if it ended up as an apology gift for Rania—or his mother— but he sure didn't want to ride into town smelling like he skinny dipped in a perfume factory vat.

When he started to walk out of the house, Jacob automatically reached for his hat on the wall peg, and then remembered again where he had left it. Looking down the row of pegs he saw his pa's old hat. His ma wore it a lot the first months after he died. She said it helped her think out problems they would have faced together. Ma went back to her own head gear eventually but Pa's hat always had an honored spot on the wall.

Jacob reverently took the hat down and thumbed the brim, thinking about his parents.

Marriage is a wonderful thing and I cherished the years I had with your father. Rania will make a fine wife, but you're going to have to accept her as she is first.

His ma's words were banging around his head again. Maybe wearing Pa's hat for a while would help him decide what to do.

***

Rania wiped her face again with the towel she'd been crying into the last hour after Jacob left. She still played their conversation over and over in her mind. He didn't give her a chance to explain what happened. Jacob thought she had let him

Brides with Grit

down by his not being her first, and she doubted Jacob would ever forgive her, let alone accept her baby.

She rubbed her tummy, knowing in her heart that she was indeed going to have a child—who she would love and protect like any good mother. And if Jacob didn't want them, so be it.

Rania cocked her head hearing Hilda, talking to her horse and dog as they came up the road. She was going to have to break the news to her twin now. Rania cringed, knowing what her sister's first reaction would be, but she knew Hilda's comfort and understanding would quickly follow after the initial shock.

"Hey, Sis! Rania! Come out and see our dogs checking each other out. It's hilarious."

Rania opened the door, walked out on the porch and leaned against the support post. Her dog King looked petrified as Hilda's ten–pound mop of a dirty white dog—fittingly named Miss Terror—barked and ran circles around his one hundred fifty pound body. That little dog was the main reason that Rania didn't mind Hilda moving to her own place—although Rania would never tell her that. Her sister loved that little dog and it just fit with Hilda's personality. At least the scene between the two dogs made her smile instead of cry.

Hilda hopped off Nutcracker and looped his reins around the front hitching post. Dressed in her usual men's trousers, shirt, vest, and spurred boots, Hilda could pass for a man with her tall beanpole figure—until she swung her waist–long braid across her shoulder—which always had a tiny pink satin ribbon tied on its end.

"Why you looking so weepy–eyed today? Missing Momma and Poppa?" Hilda asked as she stomped her way up the steps and sat down on the rocker Rania had recently moved out onto the

Rania Ropes a Rancher

porch. Rania scooted the other chair on the porch to face Hilda before sitting down.

"We need to talk, Hilda. I've been keeping something from you. I'm sorry I did it, but I just needed to come to terms with it first."

Both of Hilda's feet hit the floorboards as she grabbed Rania's hands. "We've never kept secrets from each other …but I've been feeling like something's been bothering you."

"I'm pretty sure, now, that I'm going to have a baby." Rania sighed with relief now that she had told her twin.

"What? How? When? You and Jacob haven't…" Hilda struggled to ask.

"No, not Jacob. Before that…when we were driving cattle up here. It happened before we left Texas." Rania squeezed her eyes shut with the vile memory of that horrible night. "Hilda, Sid Narker threatened to kill all of you if I…didn't do what he wanted."

"Why didn't you slug him in the groin right then and there?"

"I couldn't Hilda…"

"Yes you could have. We've always known how to fight, living with our big brothers and surviving out on the trail," Hilda announced, accusing Rania of not fighting back like she should have.

"Remember his 'Yellowbelly' Henry repeating rifle?"

"Yes, he bragged about it and tossed cartridges in his hand around us girls all the time."

Brides with Grit

"Well, one night we went up on a hill above the camp and I thought he was going to kiss me. Instead he showed me how we could see our whole family, within range, around the campfire. And he loaded the rifle, one cartridge at a time, saying 'this one's for your momma, this one's for your poppa...' until he got down to a cartridge for you. Then he kept loading, rattled off our hands' and horses' names until the rifle was full of rounds."

"I can't believe..." Hilda interrupted.

"The man was crazy and would have done it! After he...violated me...Sid told me to go back to camp, and if anybody so much as looked up at him, he'd start shooting. And remember every night after that, he'd find a place after supper to 'keep watch' he'd say, so I wouldn't tell anyone what he'd done to me."

Rania studied her twin's face as Hilda's mind replayed their trail days during this last trip. Hilda's eyes grew wide and her mouth dropped open in horror when she realized it was true. "Oh Rania, I'm so sorry. Why didn't I realize what was going on?"

"I kept it a secret to keep you all safe. I love you and want didn't you to be hurt next."

Hilda got out of the rocker and kneeled to give Rania a tight hug. Their wet cheeks were pressed together, giving each other comfort and strength.

"Thank you, Hilda, for slugging him with that limb when he cornered me again. But even after Narker left, I was so afraid he'd come back some night and start shooting."

Hilda leaned back and wiped the tears running down Rania's cheeks. "No wonder you got so thin on the trip. You were too scared to keep food down and tired from watching over us at night.

Rania Ropes a Rancher

Oh Rania, I'm so sorry you thought you had to carry this burden alone."

"I just couldn't bear to think I would be the cause of any of you coming to harm if I didn't do as he demanded."

"Well I thank you, dear sister, and now that we've moved to Kansas, you can sweep Sid Narker out of your mind," Hilda said trying to ease Rania's fears and worries.

"Not that simple, because I'm gaining weight and will be showing soon."

"And here I was getting jealous because you were filling out, growing a chest, and catching good–looking Jacob's attention."

Rania squeezed her eyes shut, trying to keep her tears from flowing again. "Jacob told me today that he wanted to court me. I had to tell him I was having a baby. He had a right to know, but he left mad, without letting me explain how it happened."

"He'll come around because I'm pretty sure he loves you, Rania. Jacob's a good man, and he'll support you."

"Jacob looked at me in disgust, like I was lower class than a saloon girl who made her living working upstairs."

"Fine. Then Jacob's not good enough for you if he can't show any compassion for what you had to do. Remember our whole family will be around to help with your baby."

"Yes, but I was ready for my own home, a husband and family. I don't want to keep living with our parents. And what will people say when I walk through town—pregnant with no husband?"

Hilda snorted in disbelief, "In this town—which has a whole lot more bachelors than available women? Before you could walk a

Brides with Grit

block with a sign saying 'I'm pregnant and want to marry you', you'd have a half–dozen proposals to pick from."

Rania laughed at the picture of her about nine months along and waddling down the street with Hilda's idea of a sign. "Well at least you've gotten me out of my crying spell. I'll just have to do my best for my baby."

"Oh, what if you have twins like us?" Hilda was jumping up and down with excitement now.

"Please, no!" Rania groaned after covering her face with her hands. "I don't know how Momma survived raising the two of us." *And how would I survive if I had two spitfire twins like Hilda at the same time?*

Well, she'd plan for what she knew was coming into her life, and forget a future with Jacob. Rania's chest tightened when thinking of another woman being in Jacob's arms, but she would not settle for a man who didn't trust her judgment, nor even listen to why she had to make the choice she felt was right at the time.

"Have you eaten yet?" Rania asked Hilda.

"Yes, since it's almost two hours past noon. I know you usually lunch with Jacob so I waited until now to visit you."

"Jacob left before we ate, so there's still food sitting out on the table. And since I can't stomach the thought of food in the morning, but eat like a horse at noon, I need to eat. And gain more weight," Rania sighed.

Hilda looked over Rania when she stood up to go inside the house. "You know you're about to bust the front out of that shirtwaist, and your skirt band is looking uncomfortable. How about we go shopping in Clear Creek after you eat?" Hilda's eyes sparkled as a big grin spread across her face. Her sister might dress

Rania Ropes a Rancher

like a man to make ranch life easier, but she sure was a woman who liked to shop.

CHAPTER 7

Jacob carefully put the new bottle of Lilac Water in his saddle bag, thinking of the static the shopkeeper gave him for having to buy another one since Jacob had "dropped" the first. You'd think Mrs. Taylor would just be happy for another sale, but no…apparently it was a crime to spill a bottle of "eau de perfume" which she called the cheap bottle of toilet water. Actually, Jacob wished the store did have some fancy perfume to give Rania, but this was the best he could find in this frontier town.

Instead of swinging into the saddle and riding back to Rania's right away, he decided to walk down the block to see if Adam was in the marshal's office. He hated to admit it but he was reluctant to face Rania's cold shoulder—because he knew he definitely deserved it. Maybe Rania would soften up to his groveling after a little more time apart. Jacob knew Rania was the right woman for him, but he was going to have to win her trust again.

Adam jumped in his chair when Jacob opened the jail door, then shuffled the papers on his desk to cover a letter he was reading when Jacob came in. "Got a love note you don't want me to see, Adam?" Jacob teased.

Rania Ropes a Rancher

Adam scowled at Jacob, and then confessed, "No, I've been reading Millie Donovan's letters to Sam Larson again to try to figure out how to contact her about his demise."

"It took us only ten minutes—weeks ago—to read those letters and I know there was no way to contact her. Why are you reading them again?" Jacob had been feeling bad all afternoon, but his brother's discomfort lifted his spirits a little bit.

"Just curious," Adam said crossing his arms. "What are you doing in town in the middle of the afternoon, and why do you smell like…lilacs?"

Jacob knew Adam was going to chew him out when Adam learned he had walked out on Rania, so he took a seat on the other side of the desk to get it over. Plus, Jacob needed his brother's advice on how to make things right with Rania—and his mother, although Jacob wouldn't tell Adam all the conversation the two of them had. Jacob hurt the two most important women in his life and he needed help to get back in their good graces.

***

Rania's spirits were better by the time she and Hilda rode into town. They decided a few yards of material weren't worth hitching the horses to the wagon, so they rode Rose and Nutcracker instead.

After arriving and giving the horses drinks from the water trough by the livery, they left them in the livery during their shopping. The day was warm and the horses would enjoy the shade until they rode home. Rania walked alone to the store because Hilda was talking to the livery man about her latest horse race, and Rania wanted to spend time in the store looking at material choices.

78

Brides with Grit

Rania turned the doorknob and walked two steps through the door of Taylor's store when she heard a man talking to the storeowner's wife. The man's voice made her freeze halfway through her third step.

"Hello Mrs. Taylor. I'm on my way to the Montana Territory on this afternoon's train…"

The air was knocked out of her chest when she realized the man who attacked her two months ago was just a few feet in front of her. She turned quickly without looking at him, hoping to get out of the store before he saw her—and before she passed out from the panic that was about to overtake her body. *She thought she was safe in Kansas but he had followed her up here!*

***

Hilda opened the marshal's office door wide enough to ask, "Adam, can I take Rania into your house for a bit? She had a scare and..." Hilda stopped when she opened the door wider and saw Jacob sitting in the other chair. "Hello, Jacob," she said coolly.

"What's wrong with Rania?" Jacob asked as he stood up.

"Not your concern. Rania thought she heard Sid Narker's voice and she fainted. When she started to wake up, she threw up, so I came in here to see if we can get into your house. She's very upset, plus covered in her own vomit."

"Narker?" Adam snorted. "I know he's a slick weasel, but he's not worth fainting over."

"You know him?"

79

Rania Ropes a Rancher

"Yes," Adam answered. "Sid Narker worked at the Bar E for about a month until Elison kicked him off the place, then Sid gave the land agent guff for not letting him take over Noah's claim. Not sure where he's been the last few weeks."

"Sid came up here after he left our cattle drive?"

"Hilda. Quit screeching. What are you talking about?"

"I didn't believe Rania when she told me. Surely it's someone with the same last name! Sid is about five foot ten, and dark brown straight hair, on the long side. Didn't have a mustache or beard back then. He used to ride a mean, white gelding, and was always playing with the cartridges for his Henry rifle."

Adam looked puzzled. "Sounds like him. But did he have a fairly large scar on his right temple? Looks like he took a rough hit with something and it didn't heal right."

"I gave him that scar when I whacked him with a tree limb! He attacked Rania in Texas when we were driving cattle up here!"

"And Rania's alone in the alley while Narker's roaming around town?!" Jacob roared as he knocked over the chair he had been sitting in.

***

Rania was sitting on Adam's porch step when Jacob came running around the corner, with Adam and Hilda close behind.

"You better deputize me Adam, because I need to be legal when I kill this Narker," Jacob was seething through gritted teeth after seeing Rania looking so pale and silent.

80

Brides with Grit

"I'm missing three–fourths of a story here. What's the deal between the twins and Sid Narker?" questioned Adam.

"I'm just putting two and two together between the bits I've gotten from Rania, Ma, and now Hilda today. Rania told me this morning that she's pregnant. I stormed off without giving her a chance to explain. I'm guessing Narker raped her."

Adam stopped dead in his tracks, staring at Jacob, and then at the women huddled together on the steps. Adam squatted down by Rania and asked softly, "Rania, is Sid Narker the man who violated you?"

Rania raised her light blue eyes to Jacob—instead of Adam— and said with firm words, "Yes, and I'm pregnant because of Sid's attack."

Adam stood up, ready to head back to his office. "Jacob, take the women into my house and *stay with them*. I know what Narker looks like so I'll start looking for him. Rania, where did you hear him?"

"I was opening the door to Taylor's store and he was talking to Mrs. Taylor. I turned quickly when I heard his voice so didn't get a good look at him. I don't know if he saw me or not."

"Okay, I'll head to the store first. Again, Jacob, stay with Rania and Hilda."

"He's free to leave and hunt for Sid too, Adam. We can take care of ourselves," Hilda said as she slipped into the house behind Rania. Jacob heard the lock turn on the door, effectively keeping him from apologizing to Rania for his stupid assumptions earlier in the day.

81

Rania Ropes a Rancher

***

Adam and Jacob scoured every place in town that they could think of, but finally decided Mrs. Taylor was right. Narker told her he was leaving on the afternoon train and the train station agent confirmed a man with Narker's description had bought a train ticket.

"Rania, may I please talk to you privately before you go home?" She hadn't looked Jacob's way once when Adam told Rania and Hilda about their search for Narker. Adam suggested they eat supper at the café before they rode home—because Adam didn't keep food in the house, but the women declined.

"We'll go fetch your horses while you talk," said Adam, grabbing Hilda's hand and pulling her along to leave Jacob and Rania on the porch alone.

"I'm so sorry, Rania, that you were attacked and *so very sorry* for not listening to you this morning. I was wrong to jump to conclusions before you could explain the circumstances." Jacob stepped toward Rania like he wanted to wrap his arms around her, but she stepped back, out of his reach.

"I know you feel bad about everything now, but why couldn't you have waited for my explanation instead of just leaving mad?" Rania questioned.

"Jacob, when I said I was pregnant, you looked at me like I was the scum of the earth. Yes, I put off telling you because I was afraid of what you'd think, and you proved me right."

He felt guilty because what Rania said was true. Jacob knew in his heart that Rania wasn't a loose woman, but hadn't even taken a

Brides with Grit

second to ask about the circumstances before coming to his own snap judgment.

"But you know what? I don't care what you think of me now. I had to protect my family and I have a clear conscience because I believe they're alive because of me."

Jacob gripped his father's hat tightly in his hand, trying to imagine what his father would have said in this situation. He didn't have the years of solid marriage that his parents had when they faced a similar pain together, but he had to think of the right words to express his sorrow and love for Rania now.

Instead of his father's wisdom, Jacob heard his mother's recent words. *Tell her what's in your heart and ask her to be honest with you. Don't let the past hamper your dreams for a wife and family.*

But right now Jacob couldn't get past the problem of raising a baby who wasn't his. A child fathered by a rapist was blurring the image of his ideal family.

"Rania, again, I'm sorry for what's happened. I believe we could still have a future together, but I just need time to sort through my feelings about the baby on the way."

"I...I love you Jacob, but if you can't accept my baby, you need to leave us alone. I know you feel an obligation to check on me because of your mother's request, but it would hurt too much to see you every day, so please stay away now."

"Rania, please..."

"No, Jacob. I can look after two sheep and a dog. The horses are all out in the pasture on their own. Narker is on his way to Montana Territory, so I can breathe a little easier now and get on

Rania Ropes a Rancher

with my life." Rania looked down at her boots, down the street…anywhere but to his face while she said her piece.

Jacob felt like such a heel, but he couldn't say the three words that would make a difference to Rania. Maybe some time apart would be the best for them. But yet…when he tried to picture his perfect wife, Rania's image still came to mind. How was he going to get over his stigma about Rania's baby?

When Adam brought Duncan to the house, Jacob took the reins, and then swung up on the saddle. "Rania, can we talk again later?"

Hilda looked at him and then her sister. "I'll check on her from now on, Jacob. If we need anything we'll go over to the Bar E," Hilda softly stated.

"Actually, why don't you all leave me alone for a few days," Rania said when swinging into the saddle herself and urged Rose to a quick trot out of Clear Creek, leaving the three looking at her stiff back.

84

CHAPTER 8

The afternoon played over and over in Rania's mind as she rode Rose toward home. Rania hated to act rudely, especially to Hilda, but she had to get away. Hearing Sid's voice had unnerved her more than she cared to admit. It made her skin crawl thinking back to that night. She thought she had gotten past cringing when someone, especially Jacob, touched or kissed her, but the bad memories flooded back when she heard her attacker again.

Could she ever get over the emotional distress of that night to enjoy married life? Jacob immediately came to mind, but that dream of married life with him vanished with the confrontation that had occurred between them.

Ever since Rania was a young child, she had dreamed of being married to a handsome man and the mother to a happy family. At first she thought they would all live in a red house, with the potato field planted next to it. The dream scene changed to a wooden–framed house in the Hill Country of Texas when they moved to America. Her recent dream of living on the Wilerson ranch and raising a family with Jacob was probably unlikely now.

85

Rania Ropes a Rancher

It was a relief to be home. All she wanted to do was to crawl into bed. There was still a foul taste in her mouth from heaving her lunch into the dirt, so Rania decided to stop by the house and get a drink of water before unsaddling Rose. It would only take a minute, so she dropped the reins and went into the house. As she dipped the tin cup into the bucket of water by the dry sink in the kitchen, she glanced around the room. She stared at the flower vase on the table. How could the roses she and Jacob picked this morning have turned black already?

Rania went over to take a better look and saw the wild pink roses were gone from the vase—and dried flower stems had taken their place. She gasped because they looked like dried stems of the Texas bluebonnets Sid picked every evening for her when they were on the trail.

Before she could yank them out of the vase, throw them on the floor and grind them into dust with her boot heel, she heard a cough from behind the front door. She guessed who it was and steeled her courage to face the man who had turned her life upside down.

"Hello, Rania. Do you like the blue bonnets I brought you? I'll always think of you when I see those pretty flowers in bloom. I picked those flowers for you when I left Texas and have been saving them just for this reunion. Of course they've lost their pretty color and fragrance, but I'm sure they still bring back memories of our kisses."

Rania slowly turned to face the man she hoped to never, ever see again. His face was in the shadow so it was hard to see the injury that Hilda had inflicted on him. She hoped it pained him until his dying day. She was past scared and on to angry. This man was not going to hurt her again!

Brides with Grit

He was leaning, relaxed, on the wall behind the front door so Rania hadn't seen him when she entered the house. Instead of his favorite rifle, Sid had a six shooter in his hand—which at the moment was held across his chest, instead of aimed at her. "I was happy to see you in Taylor's Store earlier today. Too bad you didn't come on in and say hello. I've seen you many times—at a distance—through my field glass..." He smiled when he saw Rania's eyes widen, realizing he had been spying on her.

Rania tried not to shudder, thinking of Narker watching her walking around the ranch yard, playing with the dog and sheep...and taking walks hand in hand with Jacob. As much as she wished Jacob or Hilda had followed her home, she was glad they weren't in danger from this deranged man, too. But she'd have to defend herself, and her baby, alone.

She crossed her arms against her abdomen, firmly realizing she *would* protect this baby from the man across the room calmly threatening her. The baby was because of him, but only hers to love and protect. This man would never, *ever* touch a hair on his or her head.

Narker must have recognized Rania's determination not to cower because he shifted his stance to face her, now with the pistol pointing more in her general direction.

"So Rania, you assumed I was on my way to the Montana Territory. I thought it was an excellent plan to get you and your male friends off guard. And I still plan to go north, but with you accompanying me."

Rania looked around the room. Narker was too close to the door for her to run past him—and her rifle was missing from its rack. Apparently Sid had spent his time waiting for her by going

87

Rania Ropes a Rancher

through the house. He also had her knapsack, presumably packed with some of her clothing, on the floor beside his feet.

"Yes, your essentials are packed and ready for us to leave. And no, I didn't pack your derringer hiding in your unmentionables," Narker chuckled and waggled his eyebrows at her. "All that's left to do is for you to write a letter to your sister, saying you decided to take the train south to meet your parents," Narker said as he pointed to the paper, pen and inkwell positioned on the corner of the table.

Rania sighed, not seeing a way to get away from Narker, so she needed to write something in the letter that would give Hilda a hint to her dilemma. "Just what am I supposed to write?" Rania asked trying to stall for time.

"Tell your dear sister that you're homesick for Texas and want to visit one last time before coming back to Kansas with your parents. And don't bother writing it in Swedish. I know you both can write and read in English," Narker smirked.

Rania rubbed up and down on her tummy, trying to think of a way to get both of them out of this mess. She stilled her hands when she realized Narker was closely watching her.

"Say, you're rubbing your belly like a pregnant momma does. Is there a daddy I should congratulate?"

Rania felt her face turn red with his statement, terrified he'd figured out her condition.

"I'm sure you and Wilerson have played around, but you haven't been up here in Kansas very long yet." Narker paused, his eyes shifting between Rania's face and abdomen. "Are you

Brides with Grit

carrying my first born? Well, I'll be damned," an evil grin spread across his mean face.

"You know there's a judge in the next county who owes me a favor. I'm sure he'd marry us, before we head on. You always were sweet on me, so I'm sure you'll enjoy being with me again."

Rania felt like retching again, even if it was dry heaves. She couldn't pass out again though. She would figure out a way to get away from him, even if it took time to do it.

Then she noticed the silence. "Where's my dog?"

"Oh, I think he's taking a nap in the barn, after eating a nice batch of poisoned rabbit stew. And if he didn't, he's off somewhere trying to find his lost sheep…which are about a mile away."

Rania felt sick about King. He had been so loyal to her. The dear dog even walked with her and Jacob—along with the two sheep—because King couldn't let her out of his sight when she was on the ranch.

"How will I explain about my dog in Hilda's letter?"

"Don't mention it. Or, say you brought them back over to the Bar E Ranch to stay while you're gone." Sid waved the gun around impatiently. "Just write the dang letter so we can get out of here."

Rania sat down at the table, pulled the paper in front of her and uncapped the inkwell. She swallowed the lump in her throat. How could she send clues to Hilda that something was wrong? After dipping the pen in the ink and tapping the excess off the nib, she still wasn't sure what to write.

Rania Ropes a Rancher

After a moment she wrote:

My dearest Hilda Stida,

I feel I need to break away due to my current situation. I'm traveling to connect with our parents, before they start their next trail ride north. I'll see you soon.

With much love, Rania Linnaea

Sid grabbed the letter before the ink was dry to read it. "Why did you put your middle names in the letter?"

"That's how we've always signed our names to each other. It is a twin ritual between us," Rania lied. "If I didn't do that, she'd know something was wrong." Actually Hilda's middle name wasn't Stida, but that's the first Swedish name–like word she could think of to get a "d" on the same line. Rania tried to make the "s", "i" and "d" more pronounced with her ink, hoping Hilda would see she was trying to name her abductor.

Rania was glad she hadn't touched the dried blue bonnets now. She had added the twin flower name of Linnaea as her middle name to point Hilda to the Texas flower she now loathed with a passion. She took the letter from Sid's hand and set it under the vase, then put the cap on the ink well, trying to keep Sid from looking at the letter any closer.

"I need to use the privy before we go," Rania rose from her chair, hoping Sid would follow her out of the house.

"Why? Got a little derringer tucked up in the rafters in your outhouse?" Sid grinned as he shoved her sack into her middle for her to carry, and then tightly grabbed her upper arm with his left hand. His right held the cocked revolver.

90

Brides with Grit

"Get used to it," Rania hissed. "Pregnant women have to answer calls to nature very often."

Rania was mortified when Sid pushed in behind her inside the outhouse. He looked over the inside walls before stepping out. He didn't close the door so she could lock him out, but the flimsy hook latch could easily be broken if she had tried it. Almost worse was the fact she really had to relieve herself and he could hear it.

"You're done. Let's go." Sid yanked the door open while she was still tucking in her tight shirtwaist.

Rania scanned the ranch yard as they walked out in the open. She hated to see a lifeless King lying somewhere, but she looked for him anyway. The place looked so forlorn without the dog and his little flock.

Rose was by the water tank, but Rania didn't see Sid's gelding. "Where's your horse?"

"Tied conveniently behind the barn where you wouldn't have seen it when riding in." He forced her to walk behind the building first to untie his horse. It was the same mean–tempered, white gelding Sid had in Texas. The horse's ears were back when he saw them, and he jerked his head away when Sid untied the reins from the wooden fence.

"Walk to your horse, but don't get on yet," Sid warned. Rania found out why when he threw a lariat around Rose's neck, and tied the rope to his saddle pommel. "Now put your wrists together so I can hogtie them." Rania's heart sank when she realized he was going to tie her hands to the saddle pommel after she mounted, and Rose was tied to his horse's saddle.

91

Rania Ropes a Rancher

How was she going to get away from Sid and protect her baby, she thought, as they rode out of the ranch yard? Would it make any difference that the baby she carried was his? The thought made her shudder.

Rania prayed that Hilda and Dagmar ignored her wishes to stay away. But even if they came and found the note, it might not be soon enough to help her. Hoping Jacob would visit was a lost cause when she had emphatically told him to leave her alone.

CHAPTER 9

Jacob loved his father's hat, but he needed his own back. He'd get his hat off the peg inside her front door and be on his way.

Rania and Rose weren't in sight, so maybe they took a different route home, or she was in the barn brushing down Rose after unsaddling her.

After no answer to his knock, Jacob opened the door and walked into the Hamner house. As he reached for his hat, he couldn't help but look at the vase he had given Rania as his first token of love. But now, instead of a bouquet of pink prairie roses, the vase held dried flowers, and a piece of paper lay under the glass. Curious, Jacob walked to the table to look at the note. He read *"My dearest Hilda Stida"* while the paper was lying on the table, so he moved the vase to pick up and read the rest of the letter.

Jacob dropped the note on the table and looked around the room. He couldn't believe Rania could just leave a short note to Hilda and take off by herself. Did the twins meet again and quarrel after Rania left town?

Rania Ropes a Rancher

He looked back at the paper on the table. It landed so he was looking at the note upside down. There were three letters that stood out with thicker ink. Jacob turned it around and read the letters. "S, i, d." *Sid*. Was Sid Narker waiting for Rania here instead of taking the train as they assumed?

Jacob pulled and cocked his revolver before moving to peek out the front door. Jacob left Clear Creek only fifteen or twenty minutes after Rania did. Were Narker and Rania in the barn?

Jacob's gaze swung to a distant woof coming from the pasture. King was racing toward the barn, with the sheep running far behind, trying to catch up. *What the...?*

Stepping out the door and grabbing Duncan's bridle, Jacob worked his way to the barn using the horse as a shield. He didn't want his horse shot, but he wouldn't be any help to Rania if Narker picked him off with a rifle from the barn door.

He stopped in front of the barn to look at prints when no sound or motion came from the barn. Two horses, one that came around from the back side of the barn, and Rose's smaller hoof prints were visible along with two sets of boot prints, a man's and a woman's.

After thirstily lapping water from the horse tank, King trotted into the barn and sniffed around. With one look at his food bowl, King turned around and, with his back paws, threw dirt over the whole rabbit carcass that lay in it. Jacob thought back to noon meals he had eaten with Rania. If she was cooking a rabbit for King, it was cut up in bite size–pieces and the meat tender enough for a person to eat, let alone the dog.

The first sheep raced into the barn, bleating in panic. The second sheep, limping, was slower coming into the yard. Where

94

Brides with Grit

had the sheep gone and just now coming back? Then Jacob noticed the chewed off rope dangling around the second sheep's neck. The tip of the frayed rope was a bright bloody red. Jacob looked at King again and noticed his gums were bleeding, even after he had gotten a drink of water.

So Narker had been here a while, getting rid of King and the sheep so the dog couldn't help Rania. Jacob bet that rabbit was poisoned and if that didn't kill King, Narker knew the dog would go looking for his lost flock.

Well, now Jacob needed to find the third member of "King's flock" before it was too late.

King sniffed around the footprints, searching for clues to find his mistress. Jacob was caught off guard and scrambling to get on Duncan when King let out a howl and took off north around the house and toward the river.

Now Jacob could see the hoof prints every now and then and knew which direction the horses were going. Luckily, for tracking purposes, there had been a good thunderstorm last night, creating soft earth for the horses to leave hoof prints.

Then King dropped to the ground near the river, listening intently to something. There had been a large amount of rain upstream last night causing the river here, downstream, to swell to the top of its banks. Did Narker try crossing the dangerous water? Besides the swift current, there were old trees down underwater that didn't show with the higher water level.

The dog took off forward again in a crouched position, as though he was sneaking up on a rabbit. Jacob kneed Duncan to catch up as he pulled his rifle free from the scabbard.

95

Rania Ropes a Rancher

Jacob quickly scanned the river scene when they stopped at the river bank. His heart almost stopped when he saw the horses in the middle of the flooded river that had swelled to over sixty feet wide. Narker's white horse was ahead, swimming hard but not making much headway in the swift current. Rose was struggling to keep her head above water. That's when Jacob noticed there was a rope tight around Rose's neck, leading to the other horse's saddle. The horse's air supply was getting cut off besides her struggling to swim!

Then a wave of water and debris knocked Rania's legs from the saddle but she didn't let go of the saddle horn. Jacob realized that Rania's hands were tied to the saddle—and she would go down with the horse if Rose couldn't get across.

Jacob watched the horrifying scene, trying to figure out how to get across the river without endangering Duncan and himself too. There was a bridge across the river at Ellsworth, but he'd lose them in the time it would take to make the several-mile trip. Then he spied the root end of a large, old cottonwood tree drifting down the middle of the current behind the horses. Jacob cupped his hands and screamed, "Watch out behind you!"

Both Narker and Rania turned their heads looking for the shout and saw the tree bearing down on them. Narker's hands slacked on Rose's rope in surprise, long enough to put some distance between the two horses.

The tree floated faster downstream than the horses trying to cross against the current. When the tree passed between the two horses, the upright tree roots snagged their connecting rope, jerking the horses' heads parallel to the log. But while Rose's head was being held above water, the white horse was struggling for all its worth because it was being tugged under the tree roots.

Brides with Grit

Both people were fighting for their lives, but tangled ropes were hampering both of them. Jacob saw a flash of silver and guessed Narker was trying to cut the lead rope with his knife. Both ends of the rope were caught tight in the floating roots and he couldn't get it unwrapped off the saddle horn.

Jacob watched as the white horse's head bobbed back up, finally free to struggle its swim to the opposite river bank. Meanwhile Rose and Rania were still tethered to the floating tree. Jacob and Duncan followed the tree's course down the river as close as they could get to the bank.

The tree turned sideways for a moment when it caught in more debris at a bend in the river's course. Jacob jerked his saddle tie off his lariat and formed a circle with the rope. He didn't know if he and Duncan would be pulled into the river too, but he had to try to stop the tree if possible.

Jacob heaved his rope toward the root mass, relieved when it tangled in the upright roots. Duncan pulled back, struggling to pull the roped roots closer to the edge of the bank, but the flooded water's strong current was too much for him. Jacob reined Duncan sideways and back around a young cottonwood tree growing close to the river bank. Jacob leaned out of the saddle to wrap the rope all the way around the tree trunk and tie it in a quick knot. It wasn't a big tree, but hopefully strong enough to stabilize the tree in the river.

Now he had to get Rania, and hopefully Rose, out of the water before more debris slammed into them.

"Rania! Rania!" Rania was floating alongside Rose, but she didn't turn her head with his shouts. The mare's left side was against the mass of tree limbs so it was a good thing Rania's leg

97

Rania Ropes a Rancher

wasn't still around the horse's belly. Jacob knew Rania was still alive, as she was gasping for air. Rose had quit struggling though, and was only there because of the tangled rope that had originally tied the two horses together.

Watching the shifting debris, Jacob eased into the dangerous water, hanging on to the taut rope tied between the two trees. He had to go fifteen feet to reach Rania and then return them both back to safety. Could he manage it if she was unconscious?

"I'm coming to get you and you'll be safe in a minute," Jacob's voice trembled as he tried to talk calmly to both the woman and the horse as he approached them. But King's barking was what roused Rania's eyes open, and then a flicker of Rose's eye lid.

Jacob pulled his knife out of his belt when he reached the pair. "Rania, I'm going to cut your hands loose from the pommel. Grab around my neck and hang on tight as soon as you're free." Jacob prayed as he worked to cut the rope holding Rania's wrists. He almost dropped the knife instead of getting it back in his belt when Rania's weak attempt to reach his neck failed. Jacob pulled one arm around his neck and then the other, urging her to hang on to him, as he fought to grip the rope line and keep debris from hitting them. It was a minefield of limbs—and who knows what else— careening down the swift current into Jacob as he struggled to pull them back across the raging river.

"Cough it up, Rania. You need to get this nasty water out of your lungs," Jacob hoarsely whispered after they both lay safely on the muddy river bank. Jacob couldn't remember ever being so petrified by something he had to do. He lay back on the damp ground, thankful that he had succeeded in getting them out of the water.

Brides with Grit

Jacob finally pushed King out of the way because he was trying to lick Rania's face and lay on her, as if trying to protect her. The three of them were a sopping wet, muddy mess but finally safe.

"Rose?" whispered Rania, even though she still had her eyes closed.

"Don't know. She's breathing, but tangled up in the tree debris." God he hated seeing the horse suffer, but was chicken to shoot her in front of Rania.

Jacob struggled to his feet. "I'm going back out to cut the ropes around her and get the rope off the tree. Maybe she'll float out of the mess if she can." Jacob held on to the rope again, easing out to the stranded horse. Besides cutting the lariat around her neck, he reached down the right side of her belly to cut the cinch and strap off the saddle. Jacob tried pulling the saddle off her back, but it was wedged tight between her left side and the tree. Lastly, he worked the bridle off her head and the bit out of her mouth. It was up to fate and Rose whether she lived. He couldn't tell if her legs were tangled in debris underwater.

Jacob worked his way up to the tree roots and loosened the loop that connected the tree in the water, to the tree on the bank. He thought about looping the rope about Rose and trying to pull her out, but there was so much debris in the river that he was afraid she'd wind up tangled up in the rope again. "Sorry, Rose," he choked out as he pulled himself out of the water.

Rania sobbed as she looked at Rose one last time, and then let Jacob help her into Duncan's saddle. Jacob barely mounted behind her when she fell forward from exhaustion.

Rania Ropes a Rancher

Before Jacob turned Duncan toward the ranch, he saw four white, stiff legs of an upside down horse float by in the center current. Jacob hoped Narker was still in that horse's saddle.

CHAPTER 10

He needed to get Rania out of her dirty, wet clothes, into a hot bath and put her to bed. He knew her body had to be covered with scratches and bruises, because he could feel them on his own body, and he wasn't in the water very long.

But he hated to bring all this mud and water into the house.

"Rania? I'm setting you down on the porch steps for a minute." Rania wasn't much help getting off Duncan, but managed to walk the few steps to the porch. She hissed in pain as she eased down on the top step and leaned against the porch pole.

"Let me help get your boots off." Rania stuck out her first leg, watching Jacob try to yank off her wet boot as carefully as he could. His hands were covered with the slimy river mud by the time he got it off and tipped the boot to pour out water. Jacob pulled off her other boot, then his own. Next he tugged the soggy water–brown socks off their feet.

"Shucks," Jacob said as he wiped his muddy hands on his trousers. "We just as well leave these muddy clothes out here on

Rania Ropes a Rancher

the porch instead of bringing this all in. Okay, Rania?" She just nodded, so Jacob unbuttoned his vest, then stopped, thinking about what was in his vest pockets. He pulled his pocket watch out by its chain and unfastened the clasp from the vest and popped open the case. The river water hadn't ruined it. How was it still ticking?

Jacob placed his watch on the chair on the porch, and then shrugged out of his vest. He unbuttoned his muddy trousers, pushing them off his legs, trying not to transfer too much mud from his trousers to his ankle–length drawers. Worse still, was unbuttoning the buttons on his shirt placket and pulling his soggy shirt over his head. The breeze hit his wet chest, causing his flesh to shiver. Jacob threw his clothes over the porch railing to drip the worst of the water out of them.

"You're next." Rania had already eased out of her vest, but was having problems with the buttons of her shirtwaist.

"Mind if I help?" She just barely dipped her head to answer so Jacob took a deep breath and fumbled with the buttons, trying not to press into her breasts too much as he worked her blouse open. They both gasped when he pulled her shirt off. Rania from the pain and Jacob from seeing how bruised and scratched her arms and back were.

Jacob helped her stand, and as she gripped the porch post, he unbuttoned her skirt and eased it down her legs. "Step out of it and then I'll help you inside." He wasn't about to take off her chemise and drawers outside on the porch. Jacob tossed her clothes over the railing before wrapping his arm around her waist.

Rania shook uncontrollably by the time Jacob helped her sit cross–legged on the kitchen rug. It would be the warmest spot in the house once he added wood to the stove.

102

Brides with Grit

He went into the bedroom to yank a quilt from her bed to wrap her up in, but paused when he thought of his muddy hands and her dirty body. Jacob stuck his head back out the bedroom door, "Rania, are there any old blankets we could use instead of your nice quilt?"

It took Rania a few seconds to hoarsely answer him, "In the trunk at the foot of the bed."

Jacob gingerly opened the trunk latch, wishing he had stopped to wash his hands, but luckily there was on old wool blanket on top of the pile of bedding. He pulled the blanket out of the trunk and returned to the kitchen to wrap it around Rania's shoulders.

After pausing to wash his hands and arms in the basin of water on the back porch, Jacob added more wood to the wood stove to heat water for their baths. The water reservoir was full, but he'd have to haul more water in from the well.

Jacob cautiously walked barefoot out to the well, carrying a tin bucket and his boots. He dropped the well bucket dangling from the rope into the middle of the well. After hearing the bucket hit the water level he turned the crank above the well's opening to wind the rope back up. When the bucket came level to the opening of the well, Jacob grabbed the full bucket and poured the water in and over his boots. He always hated to put on wet boots, but he didn't want to track more mud than he had to while going in and out of the house as he brought in water.

All the preparations took time, but he couldn't stop because of his own exhaustion and soreness. The only other thing he did while the water was heating was walk out to the barn, take the saddle and bridle off Duncan and let the horse out in the pasture. His horse would have to wait to get rubbed down properly.

103

Rania Ropes a Rancher

Jacob noticed King's food pan still had the rabbit in it when he was walking out of the barn. He picked up the pan and put it in the tack room so it was shut away. He didn't want King to finally wolf down the meal if it was poisoned.

The last thing Jacob did before going back into the house was to take off his soggy boots and drag the tin tub from the porch into the kitchen.

***

"Can I help you get out of your underthings?" Rania just nodded to Jacob, probably hurting so badly she didn't worry about modesty now and him seeing her nude. Besides, the wet material stuck to her skin and showed all her female parts anyway. She sighed in relief when her wet undergarments were off, and again when she sunk down into the tin tub of steaming hot water that Jacob had just filled. The tears streamed down her cheeks again, like they had been doing on and off for the past hour.

"How bad do you hurt?"

"On a scale of one to ten—about twenty," Rania whispered between quiet sobs. "I feel like a tree trunk rammed my body several times, but I think my heart hurts the worst, thinking about Rose." She covered her face with her hands and started sobbing again from the stress of the kidnapping and grief for her lost horse.

Jacob knelt down beside the tub, lathered the soap in the wash rag and tried to figure out where to start on Rania's body. She had bruises turning dark everywhere and scratches on her chest, back and extremities. It looked like one branch scraped up—or down— her face, barely missing her left eye.

104

Brides with Grit

"Is it okay if I start cleaning you up?" Jacob waited for her nod before gingerly touching her face. She grimaced as the wash cloth touched a bad cut. Even though it stung, they both knew her body had to be cleaned and treated to ward off infection.

Jacob slowly soaped and rinsed her body, wishing his hands weren't so callused and rough. "I wish I would have ridden home with you this afternoon. Why didn't Adam and I realize it was a set–up?"

Rania winced again before answering. "You couldn't have guessed what he had planned. I don't know why he was obsessed with me, but all this trouble is my fault," she whimpered.

"No, Rania. *Stop. Thinking. That.* He caused all of this, *never* you."

Rania stared ahead, her hands crossed around her chest. "When he joined our group in Texas, he was so polite to everyone. Then he started seeking me out after supper, always bringing a handful of flowers—usually bluebonnets—with him. Hilda always got the attention of men, so I was happy it was finally my turn. I was thrilled when we stole behind the cook wagon and I got my first real kiss."

Jacob's hand stilled a second, realizing Rania was finally opening up to him about her attack. He slowly moved to her shoulders, thinking that was the safest place to be touching her while she talked.

"Then one evening he took me up to a pretty little knoll that overlooked the campsite and herd. The full moon made it easy to see a long way. He started kissing me, but then he got rough, not stopping when I begged him to. Then he threatened deadly harm to

105

Rania Ropes a Rancher

my family, going into detail of how he'd make it happen, if I didn't do what he wanted."

Then she fell silent, and Jacob took his time to lather and rinse her hair. Unfortunately her braid had unraveled in the river, so it was full of mud, grass and twigs. It would take a long time to comb out her waist–length hair, but Jacob would carefully do it after her bath.

"The abuse finally ended when Hilda caught the snake with his trousers down when I went to fetch water at the creek. Between a blow with a tree limb from Hilda, and my mother's cocked gun, he took off. I never told my mother or twin—back then—that it wasn't the first time Sid had unbuttoned his pants. He threatened to trail us and kill everyone if I mentioned it."

Jacob stood, picked up the towel he had earlier placed over the back of a kitchen chair, and tossed it over his shoulder. "Well, you never have to worry about Narker again since the river took care of him and his horse." He carefully helped Rania stand up in the bath tub, wrapped the towel around her body, helped her step out of the tub, and to sit down in a chair.

"Thank you for telling me, Rania. After I left here upset this morning I went straight to my ma to talk out my frustration. She told me 'Sometimes you just have to grit your teeth and do what you have to do to protect the ones you love'." Jacob gently squeezed Rania's shoulders. "I know that's what you did for your family, and I'm *proud of you* for it."

Rania nodded with just a faint smile on her lips. "Thank you, Jacob. You don't know what that means to me for you to say that."

"Feel better now?"

Brides with Grit

"Thank you for taking care of me, Jacob. I feel a little better, but I can't get the smell of that stank river water out of my nose." Jacob thought about her comment. Did the second bottle of Lilac Water get smashed in today's ruckus, or was it still intact?

Jacob looked down, realizing he was still parading around in his drawers. No wonder Rania was keeping her eyes averted. But he needed to take a bath before dressing again.

"Did you keep Sam's clothes? I need something clean to put on after my bath."

"Yes, his clothes are in the box under the bed. And please bring me my blue wrapper, too."

Stupid! Jacob thought as he retrieved her things. He had left her sitting wrapped up in a towel and hadn't thought about how she needed to cover up.

"How about I bring some food out to King while you finish drying? Can I give him a jar of canned meat from the cellar to tide him over? Surely he'd enjoy that." With her nod, Jacob opened the cellar door and went down the steps to scan the shelves for jars of beef. He grabbed two before climbing back up the stairs. He'd heat one up later for their meal.

After putting his soggy boots back on, Jacob retrieved a shovel from the barn and buried the rabbit in the manure pile behind the barn. After thoroughly washing the dog's pan, he filled it with the canned beef. The dog was going to have to make do until he could go hunting for a rabbit.

King had followed them home from the river, but Jacob forgot to shut the gate to the sheep's pen in all the rush. So after a drink

107

of water, King had taken his sheep back north, presumably to guard Rose. He knew they would come home eventually and King would find his meal then.

Duncan's saddle, thrown over the stall side earlier, didn't reek of perfume. It was hard to believe for all the hard riding and work he and Duncan had been through that day, but the bottle of Lilac Water was still intact. He could give his second betrothal gift as planned, plus clear Rania's nose of the river water.

Jacob almost dropped the bottle of Lilac Water when he walked out of the barn and looked north. The bleating sheep were almost back to the ranch yard, but what caught Jacob's surprise was King, still a distance way, dragging a saddle, and Rose slowly limping behind him.

***

"Rania! Come out here, now!"

Lord, now what was wrong? Rania pushed her way out of the chair, limped to the door and stepped outside. Jacob had his hands on his hips and a big smile on his face as he looked toward the river. Seeing her, he rushed up to the porch, practically picking up her feet and shoving them in her muddy boots.

"Come on! You've got to see this!" Jacob put his arm around her waist, helping her down the steps and around to the back of the house.

"Rose!" Rania couldn't believe it! Her horse had survived the horrible flood! "I've got to take care of her, Jacob."

But King dropped the saddle, stalked back to Rose, and turned and growled when Rania and Jacob started toward the horse.

108

Brides with Grit

"What's he doing?" Rania turned to Jacob in surprise.

"I'm guessing he's in full guard mode now. Or he feels bad that he couldn't help you—one of his flock—so he's going to be sure that Rose gets back to the barn instead."

"And why is he hauling back the saddle?"

"Maybe King thinks he's leading her with it instead of her halter. I have no clue, but I'm glad he saved the saddle too," Jacob chuckled while grinning at the peculiar scene in front of them.

Rose stopped walking, collapsed down on her side, but got her legs tucked back under her to sit up straight. King sat down in front of her like no one was going to get past him.

"Let's just leave them be. Rose may lay there an hour or two before getting up again. Once she goes back into the barn, King will settle down and we can clean and check Rose over."

Relief flooded Rania's mind, realizing that they had all survived. She was finally free of Sid's threats. She slid a hand down to her abdomen, gently rubbing it, thinking that her baby had survived and was safe now too.

Rania Ropes a Rancher

CHAPTER 11

"I just about forgot," Jacob said, as she and Jacob returned to the house. Jacob picked up a paper-wrapped package he must have set on the porch when he grabbed her boots. "I went out to the barn to retrieve this from my saddle bag and then got side tracked when I saw King and Rose."

Rania took the package that Jacob held out to her. "What is it? Feels like a glass bottle."

Jacob looked down, blushing when he said, "It's a gift for you that I've been carrying around. I hadn't found the right moment to give it to you with all that's been going on."

Rania carefully unwrapped the paper to reveal a bottle of Lilac Water. "Well its perfect timing now to clean the river smell out of my nose. Thank you Jacob. It's a thoughtful gift."

"You're welcome. You said you liked the smell of the lilac bushes around my house, so I thought …you'd enjoy it."

Rania Ropes a Rancher

Jacob paused, looking at the bottle, and Rania wondered if he was going to explain the reason for the gift, but then he seemed to change his mind. "Mind if I clean up myself now?" Jacob asked. I feel too dirty to put ointment on your scratches."

"How about I move to the bedroom and start combing through my hair while you're doing that? I'll put this Lilac Water to work, too."

Rania didn't have the strength to work on her hair, but she needed something to do while Jacob exchanged water in the tub, took off his muddy drawers and slipped into the bathtub.

If she hadn't been so distraught earlier, she wouldn't have let Jacob see her naked, but she needed help, just as simple as that. His touch was tender and sweet, worrying over her cuts and bruises. She blushed when she heard Jacob rise out of the water in the other room. He had taken a quick scrub, and would soon be seeing her body again. But she was okay with that, knowing *this* man would never hurt her.

Jacob appeared in the bedroom doorway, now wearing Sam's old clothes. They didn't quite fit, but Rania was sure he appreciated the clean and dry clothes.

"I hope you have some ointment in the pantry?" he asked.

"Yes, but I don't think it's enough to coat my body, let alone your scratches."

"We'll start with the worst cuts and go from there."

Jacob retrieved the salve, screwed off the lid and dipped his fingers into the jar while Rania walked back into the kitchen. After just a moment's hesitation, Rania took off her wrapper, laid it on

112

the table, and stuck her arms out. Jacob carefully dabbed salve here and there on her arms, before moving to her shoulders, neck and back. "Want your nightgown on now? You can do your front and legs yourself."

But his touch was a comfort to Rania even if they weren't married. "Just go ahead and finish. My fingers are stiff and sore too."

Jacob paused at the scratch across her abdomen. "Do you feel like little Linnaea is okay?"

"Who?" Rania looked up into Jacob's eyes, and then down to his hand.

Jacob smeared the salve across the scratch, and then his big hand cupped what would become her baby bump. "Um, I've been thinking of names for our baby, and thought your middle name would be nice for her first name."

Rania sucked in her breath and stared up at Jacob's face. "Actually my middle name is Marie. I wrote the wrong middle name on the letter to give Hilda a clue."

"Well, Linnaea Marie would be a beautiful name for our daughter." He had a tentative smile on his face. "I think we need to go with a flower theme." He leaned forward and gave her a petal soft kiss on her lips. "Linnaea and Lilly would match for twins, although I bet we'd end up calling them Linny and Lilly."

Rania was thrilled with Jacob's kiss and names. He was ready to commit to her and the baby. She sighed in relief that the nightmare of the last months was finally over, and realized she was ready to grasp her dream of a family again.

113

Rania Ropes a Rancher

"What if it's a boy?" Rania softly asked.

"Wilersons have a tradition of naming children after people in the Bible. I'll like our girls to be named for favorite flowers, but the boys could have strong biblical names, like Jonah or John."

"And if we have twin boys?" Rania was smiling through shining tears now.

"Of course David and Goliath comes to mind first," Jacob chuckled, "and with your luck of family, I'm sure one of our twins would turn out with Hilda's fire."

Rania covered Jacob's hand with her own and searched his eyes. "Are you sure about this? Your two conflicts with me were that I had been with a man, and had a child on the way. What changed?"

"I love you," Jacob brought her hands up to his lips for a quick kiss, "and Ma bluntly pointed out the things that happened to you were not your fault. Will you give me another chance, Rania? Can I be your husband? Please?"

Rania blushed pink and reached for her nightgown. She knew Jacob was waiting for an answer, but her sense of modesty came back, thinking about their wedding night. After Jacob helped her slip the soft, clean cloth over her sore body, she sighed—and tried not to wince as she put her hands around his neck and her lips on his. "Yes, you may," she whispered before sealing their commitment with a firm kiss.

114

CHAPTER 12

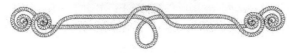

A Week Later…

Jacob stood back and looked at the wash house as he waited for Rania and Hilda to arrive to the Wilerson ranch. His last gift to Rania was done and ready for her to see. It was the week past Rania's kidnapping, but the events of that evening and the following days kept passing through his mind. Jacob wasn't going to be at peace until they were married and together.

That evening a week ago, after he—and Rania in her night gown—tended to an exhausted Rose, Jacob rode to Hilda's, who immediately rode over to stay with her twin. Only then did Jacob return to his home and get some sleep himself.

The next morning Jacob rode into Clear Creek to report Rania's kidnapping and the accident at the river. Ellsworth County lawmen scoured the river for several miles before finding Narker's horse, bloating among some jammed logs. Narker's body was not found, so they assumed he suffered the same fate as his horse. Town marshals downriver were notified so they would know the

Rania Ropes a Rancher

identity of the body if it showed up. And just in case Narker was alive, a wanted notice was also issued for his kidnapping of Rania.

Hilda spent the week with Rania, as her twin healed from her ordeal. Jacob stopped by each evening, after the day's work at his ranch. Rania boldly told Hilda to stay in the house while she and Jacob checked Rose, giving them private time for some passionate kisses and talks.

Now Jacob was ready to give his third gift to his future bride. He knew it wasn't needed, but decided Rania would enjoy his version of the Swedish tradition leading up to their betrothal, and their wedding on Sunday. Today's dinner was sort of an early Midsummer's Day theme too. Rania and Hilda talked about many of the Swedish traditions and holidays they remembered as children, so tables and chairs were set up outside between the garden and the wash house to eat the meal outside, like their Swedish summer holiday meal.

Now everything was ready and he was waiting for his bride-to-be. Hilda was to bring Rania a half hour later than the other guests so everything could be set up ahead of time. And it turned out there were two extra guests that they didn't know were coming, but his mother took it all in stride.

Isaac Connely brought his nephew Marcus Brenner, an Army officer who was visiting until his tour at Fort Hays started next month. It was interesting that Marcus and Sarah kept stealing glances at each other—when they thought the other wasn't looking—even though Ethan was deep in a conversation with Isaac, right beside the pair.

The other surprise guest was Miss Cora Elison—who arrived from Boston yesterday—without giving Dagmar any notice. Not

116

Brides with Grit

only had Cora settled into the Bar E Ranch house, but she invited herself to this family dinner, too. Cora seemed to be a spunky young woman who rattled easy–going Dagmar into stiff silence.

Still missing from the dinner was Noah, but he had wired saying he was heading home. Rania's parents also wired they would not be coming in until late summer, so Rania and Jacob decided to go ahead and get married now. Adam had stayed in town, waiting for the elusive Miss Millie Donovan who was supposed to arrive on the train this week.

Jacob and Rania decided they would live at the Hamner ranch until Rania's parents came home. Jacob would go back and forth to do chores at both places, and he and Rania could have privacy for the first weeks of their marriage.

"Hello the House!" yelled Hilda, causing Jacob to jog out to meet them, and everyone else to scramble inside the house.

"Welcome Ladies," Jacob said as he helped Rania down from the wagon.

"I'll drive the team down to the barn and be back in a minute," called Hilda as she shook the team's reins and drove away.

Jacob pulled Rania into his arms and gave her a kiss. "I gave you two gifts, the vase and the Lilac Water, and now I want to give you a third gift."

"Another one?"

Jacob wrapped his arm around Rania's waist, pulling her next to his side. "Well, I think this one will surprise you—at least I hope it will. Please close your eyes while we walk around the house and keep them shut until I say so."

117

Rania Ropes a Rancher

Rania smiled and did as he asked. Two weeks ago she would have been too scared to walk into a situation blindly, but now she was a carefree woman again. "Okay, I'm ready for my surprise!"

He guided her around to the back of the house, just at the right place so she could see everything at once. "Okay, open your eyes and tell me what you see, Rania."

"Oh, you've painted the wash house."

"What color?"

"Red."

"I'd call it Falun Red. What else do you see?"

Rania grinned at his color choice. "There are flowers around the wash house and the garden beside it."

"We'll pretend the garden is a potato field. What else?"

Rania was openly laughing now, scanning the backyard to see what else he wanted her to see.

"There's a tree sapling sitting in a bucket by the wash house. What's that supposed to mean?"

"I'm trying to create my version of the Swedish betrothal for you. When your family talked about weddings in Sweden at our first meal together, you talked about a betrothal being announced in church three Sundays in a row and about giving gifts to mark the event. So I decided to give you three gifts leading up to our marriage.

118

Brides with Grit

"The first gift was to remind you of the flowers in Sweden. It was Ma's idea to pick the flowers for the vase together so we could get to know each other better.

"The second gift represents the lilacs that will bloom around our house each year for you. I admit I was hesitant to tell you why I picked the gift at the time, because I didn't know where I stood with you then." Jacob gave her a quick kiss. "But things went well after that, didn't they?"

"Oh yes they did," Rania grinned in reply. "So, the tree is my third gift? Please tell me why."

"We don't have birch trees here like you did in Sweden, but once on our walks you said the cottonwood leaves reminded you of the Swedish birch tree leaves. And Hilda mentioned a tree is often the third gift for the Swedish betrothal."

Jacob took Rania's hand and kissed the back of it before continuing. "You once described what made a place feel like home to you. Since this ranch will always be your home, I wanted to make it special for you. I couldn't quite see painting our house red, but I hope the wash house by the garden will be a pretty place for you to remember your Swedish roots. And we'll plant the little tree wherever you want so you can watch it grow."

"I still wonder why you picked me for a wife, Jacob. Are you sure?"

Jacob faced Rania, wrapped his arms around her waist and stared into her blue eyes. "The first time I saw you, you were riding drag behind cattle trailing down Ellsworth's Main Street. You and Rose were covered in mud."

Rania Ropes a Rancher

"I remember that. We took a slide down the riverbank earlier in the day and looked a mess."

"Yes, you were muddy head to toe, even a little mud on your braid. Remember when we met later in the day on the boardwalk?"

"I looked back because I thought you were so handsome."

"And I fell off the boardwalk because I thought you were so pretty. And by watching you ride earlier, I knew you were good with horses and didn't mind a little mud. I knew right then you had roped my heart and would be the perfect rancher's wife, the perfect wife for me."

Jacob hugged Rania to his chest. "So welcome *home*, Rania," Jacob whispered as he softly kissed Rania's upturned lips.

Brides with Grit

Dear Readers: I hope you enjoyed the first book in the **Brides with Grit** series, and meeting the Wilerson and Hamer families.

My goal for this series is to honor the strong women who lived on the Kansas prairie during the frontier years. The characters and their stories were fabricated in my mind after viewing photos of real couples in my great grandparent's photo album. These 1800s photos were used for the book covers too.

The series setting is based on the famous old cowtown of Ellsworth, Kansas during its cattle drive days. The town of Clear Creek though, is fictional, based on the many little towns that sprang up as the railroad was built across Kansas.

This particular area is now the current Kanopolis State Park in central Kansas. Being local to where I live, I've hiked the park's hiking trails, where it's easy to visualize what the area looked like in 1873—because it remains the same now—as then.

Although not all of the **Brides with Grit** titles are published yet as of this book's printing, please look for the following titles on Amazon.com to find out when they are available.

Rania Ropes a Rancher (Rania Hamner and Jacob Wilerson)

Millie Marries a Marshal (Millie Donovan and Adam Wilerson)

Hilda Hogties a Horseman (Hilda Hamner and Noah Wilerson)

Cora Captures a Cowboy (Cora Elison and Dagmar Hamner)

Sarah Snares a Soldier (Sarah Wilerson and Marcus Brenner)

Cate Corrals Cattleman (Cate Wilerson and Isaac Connely)

Delia Desires a Drover (Delia Larson and Reuben Shepard)

Tina Tracks a Trail Boss (Tina Narker and Leif Hamner)

ABOUT THE AUTHOR

Linda Hubalek majored in agriculture in college, and featured in *Country Woman Magazine* about her wildflower business when her husband's job transferred them to California. She then started writing about the Kansas prairie she was homesick for and started her writing career.

Linda's first book, *Butter in the Well*, written as diary entries, is about the Swedish immigrant that homesteaded her family farm. Readers wanted to know what happened to the family, so she continued the story with *Prairie Bloomin'*, *Egg Gravy* (a pioneer cookbook), and *Looking Back*.

Her next historical fiction series features pioneer women as they experience the Civil War firsthand. *Trail of Thread*, *Thimble of Soil*, and *Stitch of Courage*, written in the form of letters, has a quilt theme because of a quilt handed down in Linda Hubalek's family. *Tying the Knot,* in the Kansas Quilter series, continues the storyline through the next generation of Pieratts.

Planting Dreams, Cultivating Hope, and *Harvesting Faith* tells her ancestor's story that changed their family history forever when they homesteaded on the unforgiving Kansas prairie.

Linda Hubalek and her husband eventually moved back home to Kansas, and she continues to write about pioneer women that made Kansas their home.

www.LindaHubalek.com

www.Facebook.com/LindaHubalekbooks

Linda Hubalek's Amazon Page

Brides with Grit

Historical Fiction by <u>Linda K. Hubalek</u>

Trail of Thread

A Woman's Westward Journey, Historical Letters 1854-1855

Trail of Thread Series, Book 1

Taste the dust of the road and feel the wind in your face as you travel with a Kentucky family by wagon train to the new territory of Kansas in 1854.

Find out what it was like for the thousands of families who made the cross-country journey into the unknown.

In this first book of the *Trail of Thread* series; in the form of letters she wrote on the journey, Deborah Pieratt describes the scenery, the everyday events on the trail, and the task of taking care of her family. Stories of humor and despair, along with her ongoing remarks about camping, cooking, and quilting on the wagon trail make you feel as if you pulled up stakes and are traveling with the Pieratt's, too.

But hints of the brewing trouble ahead plagued them along the way as people questions their motive for settling in the new territory. If they are from the South, why don't they have slaves with them? Would the Pieratt's vote for or against legal slavery in the new state? Though Deborah does not realize it, her letters show how this trip affected her family for generations to come.

This series is based on author Linda K. Hubalek's ancestors that traveled from Kentucky to Kansas in 1854.

123

Thimble of Soil

A Woman's Quest for Land, Historical Letters 1854-1860

Trail of Thread Series, Book 2

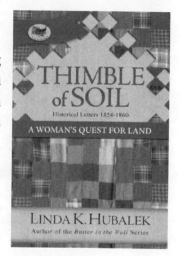

Experience the terror of the fighting and the determination to endure as you stake a claim alongside the women caught in the bloody conflicts of Kansas in the 1850's.

Follow the widowed Margaret Ralston Kennedy (a relative of the author) in this second book of the *Trail of Thread* series, as she travels with eight of her thirteen children from Ohio to the Territory of Kansas in 1855.

Thousands of Americans headed west in the decade before the Civil War, but those who settled in Kansas suffered through frequent clashes between proslavery and free-state fractions that gripped the territory.

Told through her letters, *Thimble of Soil* describes the prevalent hardships and infrequent joys experienced by the hardy pioneer women of Kansas, who struggled to protect their families from terrorist raids while building new homes and new lives on the vast unbroken prairie.

Margaret was dedicated to the cause of the North, and while the male members of her family were away fighting for a free state, she valiantly defended their homestead and held their families together through the savage years of Bleeding Kansas.

Stitch of Courage

A Woman's Fight of Freedom, Historical Letters 1861-1865

Trail of Thread Series, Book 3

Feel the uncertainty, doubt, and danger faced by the pioneer women as they defend their homes and pray for their men during the Civil War.

Stitch of Courage, the third book in the *Trail of Thread* series, tells the story of the orphaned Maggie Kennedy, who followed her brothers to Kansas in the late 1850s.

The niece of Margaret Ralston Kennedy, the main character in Hubalek's *Thimble of Soil* book, Maggie married the son of Deborah Pieratt, whose story was told in the Hubalek's *Trail of Thread* book.

In letters to her sister in Ohio, Maggie describes how the women of Kansas faced the demons of the Civil War, fighting bravely to protect their homes and families while never knowing from one day to the next whether their men were alive or dead on the faraway battlefield.

We think the Civil War took place in the South, but the Plains States endured their share of battles and tragedy. Not only did Kansas and Missouri experience a resurgence in the terrorist raids that plagued them in the years before the war, the Confederate Army tried several times to sweep across the Great Plains and capture the West.

Butter in the Well

A Scandinavian Woman's Tale of Life on the Prairie, 1868-1888

Butter in the Well Series, Book 1

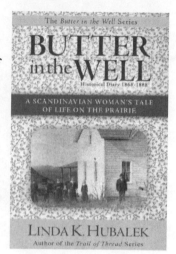

Read the fictionalized account of Kajsa Svenson Runeberg, an emigrant wife who recounts, through her diary, how she and her family built up a farm on the unsettled Kansas prairie from 1868 to 1888.

This historical fiction is based on the actual Swedish woman who homesteaded the author's childhood home and is the first of the four-book *Butter in the Well* series.

"...could well be the most endearing 'first settler' account ever told. Once a reader starts the book, they are compelled to keep reading to see what will happen next on the isolated prairie homestead. Not to be missed! — *Capper's Family Bookstore*

Hubalek has skillfully blended fiction and historic fact to recreate the life of Swedish homestead, Kajsa Svensson Runeberg. A story of emigrant dreams and pioneer struggles, it is an altogether rewarding story and one that deserves to be told. — *Kansas State Historical Society*

Prairie Bloomin'

The Prairie Blossoms for an Immigrant's Daughter, 1889-1900

Butter in the Well Series, Book 2

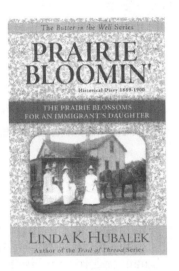

Popular Kansas author Linda K. Hubalek continues the story of a Swedish immigrant family featured in the *Butter in the Well* series with the second book *Prairie Bloomin'* (formerly titled *Prärieblomman*).

Prairie Bloomin' features the 1889 to 1900 diary of daughter Alma Swenson, as she grows up on the farm her parents homesteaded.

Even though born on the same farm in two different centuries, Prairie Bloomin's main character, Alma Swenson Runneberg, and the author shared uncanny similarities while growing up in the Smoky Valley region of central Kansas. Both the third child of their families, they lived in the same house, played in the same yard and worked the same acres until each married and moved off the farm.

"…is a tender and touching diary…Hubalek has succeeded in blowing life into both Alma and the fascinating times she lived through. Hubalek's books give Swedish-Americans a perspective of the past." *Anders Neumueller, Swedish Press, Vancouver, BC Canada*

Egg Gravy

Authentic Recipes from the Butter in the Well Series

Butter in the Well Series, Book 3

Faded recipes. We've all come across them from time to time in our lives, either handwritten by ourselves or by another person in our family, or as old yellowed newspaper clippings stuck in a cookbook of sorts.

While doing research for the *Butter in the Well* series, the author found old recipes and home remedies along with family and community histories.

These recipes had been handwritten in old ledger books, on scraps of paper, in the margins of old cookbooks and forever etched in the memories of those pioneer women's children that Linda Hubalek interviewed.

As a result, *Egg Gravy* is a collection of recipes the pioneer women used during their homesteading days. Most of the recipes can be traced back to the original women that homesteaded the real-life setting of *Butter in the Well*. Antique family photos add a personal feel to the cookbook.

From Green Pumpkin Pie, Caramel Ice Cream, and Smoked Pig Paunch to Christine's Fruit Cake, Apple Sauce Cake, and Rhubarb Marmalade, these are culinary samplings of a yesteryear that would grace any menu today. — *Midwest Book Review*

Looking Back

The Final Tale of Life on the Prairie, 1919

Butter in the Well Series, Book 4

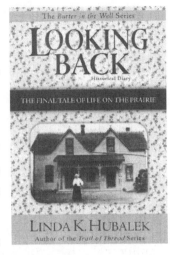

The inevitable happens—time moves on and we grow older. Instead of our own little children surrounding us, grandchildren take their place.

Each new generation lives in a new age of technology, not realizing the changes the generations before theirs has seen-and improved for them.

The cycle of life has change the prairie also. Endless waves of tall native prairie grass have been reduced to uniform rows of grain crops. The curves of the river have shifted over the decades, eroded by both man and nature. The majestic prairie has been tamed over time.

In this fourth book of the *Butter in the Well* series, Kajsa Svensson Runeberg, now age 75, looks back at the changes she has experienced on the farm she homesteaded 51 years ago. She reminisces about the past, resolves the present situation, and looks toward their future off the farm.

Don't miss this heart-rending touching finale!

Planting Dreams

A Swedish Immigrant's Journey to America, 1868-1869

Planting Dreams Series, Book 1

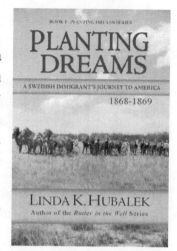

Can you imagine starting a journey to an unknown country in 1868, not knowing what the country would be like, where you would live, or how you would survive? Did you make the right decision to leave in the first place?

This first book in the *Planting Dreams* series portrays Swedish immigrant Charlotta Johnson (author Linda Hubalek's ancestor), as she ponders the decision to leave her homeland, travel to America, and worries about her family's future in a new country.

Each chapter is written as a thought-provoking story as the family travels to a new country to find a new life.

Why did this family leave? Drought scorched the farmland of Sweden and there was no harvest to feed families or livestock. Taxes were due and there was little money to pay them. But there were ships sailing to America, where the government gave land to anyone who wanted to claim a homestead.

Follow Charlotta and her family as they travel by ship and rail from Sweden, to their homestead on the open plains of Kansas.

Cultivating Hope

Homesteading on the Great Plains, 1869-1886

Planting Dreams Series, Book 2

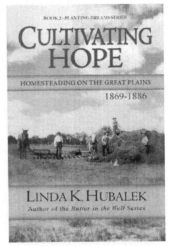

Can you imagine being isolated in the middle of treeless grassland with only a dirt roof over your head? Having to feed your children with whatever wild plants or animals you could find living on the prairie?

Sweating to plow the sod, plant the seed, cultivate the crop—only to lose it all by a hailstorm right before you harvest it?

This second book in the *Planting Dreams* series portrays Swedish immigrant Charlotta Johnson as she and her husband build a farmstead on the Kansas prairie.

This family faced countless challenges as they homestead on America's Great Plains during the 1800s. Years of hard work develop the land and improve the quality of life for her family—but not with a price.

Readers compare Hubalek's books as a combination of Laura Ingalls Wilder's *Little House on the Prairie* books, *The Emigrants* series by Vilhelm Moberg, and a Willa Cather novel.

Harvesting Faith

Life on the Changing Prairie, 1886-1919

Planting Dreams Series, Book 3

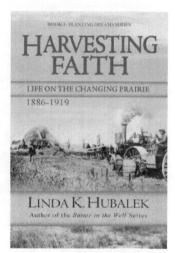

Imagine surveying your farmstead on the last day of your life, reviewing the decades of joys, hardships, and changes that have taken place on the eighty acres you have called home for the past fifty years. Would you feel at peace or find remorse at the decisions that took place in your life?

This third book in the *Planting Dreams* series portrays Charlotta Johnson as she recalls the events that shaped her family's destiny. A mixture of fact and fiction, based on the author's family, this book reviews the events that shaped this Swedish immigrants family as her children reached adulthood and had families of their own.

Join Charlotta as she reminisces about the important places and events in her past as she bids farewell to her mortal life on the Kansas prairie.

Order Form- Photocopy or Tear Out Page

Order to: Butterfield Books Inc., PO Box 407, Lindsborg KS 67456

Orders: **1-785-227-9250**   Email: **staff@ButterfieldBooks.com**

Order online at www.ButterfieldBooks.com

Send to:

Name _____

Address _____

Town, St_____ Zip _____

☐ **Check** enclosed, payable to **Butterfield Books Inc.**

☐ **Charge my credit card**

_____Exp_____CVV _____

Signature _____

Title	Qty	Unit	Total
Butter in the Well		11.95	
Prairie Bloomin'		11.95	
Egg Gravy		11.95	
Looking Back		11.95	
Butter in the Well Series (4 bks)		42.95	
Trail of Thread		11.95	
Thimble of Soil		11.95	
Stitch of Courage		11.95	
Trail of Thread Series (3 bks)		32.95	
Planting Dreams		11.95	
Cultivating Hope		11.95	
Harvesting Faith		11.95	
Planting Dreams Series (3 bks)		32.95	
Tying the Knot		11.95	
Rania Ropes a Rancher		11.95	
		Subtotal	
	KS	add 8.65% tax	
S/H per address: $3.00 for 1st book, Each add'l $.50			
		Total	

134

Order Form- Photocopy or Tear Out Page

Order to: Butterfield Books Inc., PO Box 407, Lindsborg KS 67456

Orders: **1-785-227-9250**   Email: **staff@ButterfieldBooks.com**

Order online at www.ButterfieldBooks.com

Send to:

Name _____

    Address _____

    Town, St_____ Zip _____

    ☐ **Check** enclosed, payable to **Butterfield Books Inc.**

    ☐ **Charge my credit card**

    # _____Exp____CVV _____

    Signature _____

Title	Qty	Unit Price	Total
Butter in the Well		11.95	
Prairie Bloomin'		11.95	
Egg Gravy		11.95	
Looking Back		11.95	
Butter in the Well Series (4 bks)		42.95	
Trail of Thread		11.95	
Thimble of Soil		11.95	
Stitch of Courage		11.95	
Trail of Thread Series (3 bks)		32.95	
Planting Dreams		11.95	
Cultivating Hope		11.95	
Harvesting Faith		11.95	
Planting Dreams Series (3 bks)		32.95	
Tying the Knot		11.95	
Rania Ropes a Rancher		11.95	
		Subtotal	
	KS add	8.65% tax	
S/H per address: $3.00 for 1st book, Each add'l $.50			
		Total	

136

Made in the USA
San Bernardino, CA
21 October 2014